Barbara C..ist,
who is also an historian, playwright, lecturer, political speaker
and television personality, has now written over 589 books and
sold over 600 million copies all over the world.

She has also had many historical works published and has
written four autobiographies as well as the biographies of her
mother and that of her brother, Ronald Cartland, who was the
first Member of Parliament to be killed in the last war. This book
has a preface by Sir Winston Churchill and has just been
published with an introduction by the late Sir Arthur Bryant.

"Love at the Helm" a novel written with the help and
inspiration of the late Earl Mountbatten of Burma, Great Uncle
of His Royal Highness The Prince of Wales, is being sold for the
Mountbatten Memorial Trust.

She has broken the world record for the last nineteen years by
writing an average of twenty-three books a year. In the Guinness
Book of Records she is listed as the world's top-selling author.

In 1978 she sang an Album of Love Songs with the Royal
Philharmonic Orchestra.

In private life Barbara Cartland, who is a Dame of Grace of
the Order of St John of Jerusalem, Chairman of the St John
Council in Hertfordshire and Deputy President of the St John
Ambulance Brigade, has fought for better conditions and salaries
for Midwives and Nurses.

She championed the cause for the Elderly in 1956 invoking a
Government Enquiry into the "Housing Conditions of Old
People".

In 1962 she had the Law of England changed so that Local
Authorities had to provide camps for their own Gypsies. This
has meant that since then thousands and thousands of Gypsy
children have been able to go to School which they had never
been able to do in the past, as their caravans were moved every
twenty-four hours by the Police.

There are now fourteen camps in Hertfordshire and Barbara
Cartland has her own Romany Gypsy Camp called Barbaraville
by the Gypsies.

Her designs "Decorating with Love" are being sold all over the USA and the National Home Fashions League made her in 1981 "Woman of Achievement".

Barbara Cartland's book "Getting Older, Growing Younger" has been published in Great Britain and the USA and her fifth Cookery Book, "The Romance of Food" is now being used by the House of Commons.

In 1984 she received at Kennedy Airport, America's Bishop Wright Air Industry Award for her contribution to the development of aviation. In 1931 she and two RAF Officers thought of, and carried, the first aeroplane-towed glider air-mail.

During the War she was Chief Lady Welfare Officer in Bedfordshire looking after 20,000 Service men and women. She thought of having a pool of Wedding Dresses at the War Office so a Service Bride could hire a gown for the day.

She bought 1,000 secondhand gowns without coupons for the ATS, the WAAFS and the WRENS. In 1945 Barbara Cartland received the Certificate of Merit from Eastern Command.

In 1964 Barbara Cartland founded the National Association for Health of which she is the President, as a front for all the Health Stores and for any product made as alternative medicine.

This has now a £600,000,000 turnover a year, with one third going in export.

In January 1988 she received "La Medaille de Vermeil de la Ville de Paris", (The Gold Medal of Paris). This is the highest award to be given by the City of Paris for ACHIEVEMENT – 25 million books sold in France.

In March 1988 Barbara Cartland was asked by the Indian Government to open their Health Resort outside Delhi. This is almost the largest Health Resort in the world.

Barbara Cartland was received with great enthusiasm by her fans, who also fêted her at a Reception in the City and she received the gift of an embossed plate from the Government.

Barbara Cartland was made a Dame of the Order of the British Empire in the 1991 New Year's Honours List, by Her Majesty The Queen, for her contribution to literature and for her work for the Community.

Dame Barbara has now written the greatest number of books by a British author, passing the 564 books written by John Creasey.

AWARDS

1945   Received Certificate of Merit, Eastern Command.

1953   Made a Commander of the Order of St John of Jerusalem. Invested by H.R.H. The Duke of Gloucester at Buckingham Palace.

1972   Invested as Dame of Grace of the Order of St John in London by The Lord Prior, Lord Cacia.

1981   Receives "Achiever of the Year" from the National Home Furnishing Association in Colorado Springs, U.S.A.

1984   Receives Bishop Wright Air Industry Award at Kennedy Airport, for inventing the aeroplane-towed Glider.

1988   Receives from Monsieur Chirac, The Prime Minister, the Gold Medal of the City of Paris, at the Hôtel de la Ville, Paris, for selling 25 million books and giving a lot of employment.

1991   Invested as Dame of the Order of The British Empire, by H.M. The Queen at Buckingham Palace, for her contribution to literature.

Love and a Cheetah

Ilesa Harle and her Father the Hon. Mark Harle who is the Vicar of Littlestone are finding it difficult to 'make ends meet'.

When he has left to see a prisoner who is sick, Ilesa's half-sister Doreen arrives unexpectedly after having neglected her family for some years.

She married an elderly Peer who was very rich but who died. Now she is determined to marry the handsome Duke of Mountheron who is staying with friends not far from the Vicarage.

The Vicar has been left two fine and unusual pictures by Stubbs and as the Duke is a keen collector of Stubbs' pictures Doreen has invited him to come to see them.

However, she has been staying the previous night at an Inn with an 'old Flame' who is madly in love with her. They were seen by one of her enemies – a man she knows will undoubtedly tell the Duke what he has discovered.

This will ruin Doreen's chances of marrying him.

She begs Ilesa to convince the Duke that she has been staying at the Vicarage for some days and to make sure her Father is told this when he returns.

The Duke arrives at the Vicarage and is so thrilled with the Stubbs pictures that he invites the Vicar and his daughters to go with him to Heron to see his collection.

Doreen because she is jealous hopes to prevent her sister from accepting, but the Duke insists.

How Ilesa discovers the Duke's secret when she is walking in his garden.

How the Duke finds her in what could be a very dangerous situation.

And how the Duke falls in love with Ilesa, but her half-sister casts a shadow over their happiness is all told in this enchanting story, the 495th by Barbara Cartland.

BARBARA CARTLAND

Love and a Cheetah

Mandarin

A Mandarin Paperback

LOVE AND A CHEETAH

First published in Great Britain 1994
by Mandarin Paperbacks
an imprint of Reed Consumer Books Ltd
Michelin House, 81 Fulham Road, London SW3 6RB
and Auckland, Melbourne, Singapore and Toronto

A CIP catalogue record for this title
is available from the British Library

ISBN 0 7493 1281 5

Printed and bound in Great Britain
by Cox & Wyman Ltd, Reading, Berkshire

AUTHOR'S NOTE

Stubbs was one of the greatest of English painters.

For some time he was underrated by being labelled 'Mr. Stubbs, the Horse Painter'.

Gradually however, people began to realise how important he was and he achieved equal recognition with his contemporaries, Reynolds and Gainsborough in the foremost rank of British Art.

No one but Stubbs has the originality of his paintings of animals and he also had a similar genius in his portraiture of human beings.

Sportsmen have collected Stubbs ever since he first started to paint horses. The Queen and other members of the Royal Family have his paintings in their collections.

The Cheetah, which Stubbs also portrayed so brilliantly in a picture, is the fastest mammal in the world over a short distance.

The name 'Cheetah' originated in India and means 'The Spotted One'.

In history, the Cheetah was used as an emblem on the reliefs and friezes of the Ancient Egyptians where they exemplified courage.

There are records of the Cheetah being a Royal pet of Genghis Khan and the Emperor Charlemagne.

For many years Indian Princes used to hunt with them, training them to run up game, but since 1930 there is no record of a Cheetah living wild in India, and they exist only in Africa.

The Cheetah purrs like a cat when he is pleased and happy – his whole body vibrating like an engine.

They will lick the face of anyone they like, but to nibble someone's ear is a sign of great affection.

A recent census has found that while the Cheetah is still to be found in certain parts of Africa, they will only survive if they are protected.

CHAPTER ONE
1878

Ilesa finished arranging the flowers in the Church and thought they looked very lovely.

It had been a joy to have so many now that it was May.

There were not only the Spring flowers, but also those that bloomed at the beginning of the Summer.

She took a last look round the little Norman Church in which she had been baptised by her Father, and confirmed.

She then walked towards the door.

There she stopped to look back and admire the altar with the Arum Lilies which had come from the garden.

There were also some golden azaleas.

She knew the person who would have appreciated them most would have been her Mother.

She could never remember a time when every room in the Vicarage had not been filled with flowers.

Because the people in the village had loved her Mother, they had always brought her the first flowers that came out in their small gardens.

Shutting the Church door, Ilesa walked from the porch down past the ancient tomb-stones.

Beyond this was the Lychgate which led into the Park.

Far away in the distance she could see a glimpse of Harlestone Hall where her Father had been born and brought up.

The 6th Earl of Harlestone as regards his three sons had kept to tradition.

Robert, his eldest son, who would inherit the title had gone into the family Regiment.

Henry, his second son, had entered the Royal Navy as a Midshipman, and had risen by sheer merit to gain command of a Destroyer.

Mark, his third son, following tradition went into the Church and was offered the choice of any of the livings on the Harlestone Estate.

The Honourable Mark Harle had accepted the situation because it was what he had been brought up to expect.

He had also, unfortunately, accepted his Father's decision as to whom he should marry.

The Earl had chosen for his eldest son the daughter of an important Peer, who had money of her own.

His second son had refused to be hurried up the aisle and had managed to remain unmarried.

He, however, lost his life in a battle at sea when his Destroyer was sunk.

Mark had married when he was only twenty-two.

His bride was the daughter of a man who found

Harlestone Hall and the Earl himself very impressive.

The young couple had nothing in common and had been unhappy from the very start.

Although no one said so openly, it had been a relief when after six years of arguing and wrangling with each other, she had, one exceptionally cold Winter, contracted pneumonia from which she did not recover.

She had left behind her a daughter aged five who had grown up to be very like her Mother.

Once Mark was free and the prescribed year of mourning had ended, he wasted no time.

He was now the Vicar of Littlestone and married the girl he had always loved, but had been too shy to approach.

She was the daughter of a neighbouring Country Squire, and they had met at the parties given by their parents.

Elizabeth was so beautiful that he had been convinced she would never look in his direction.

However she had in fact loved him ever since she had been a child.

Elizabeth had managed to remain unmarried.

Her parents were too fond of their daughter to force her into doing anything against her inclinations.

Elizabeth and Mark were married very quietly.

After an ecstatic honeymoon they settled down in Littlestone to make the village a happy place.

Their daughter Ilesa was born a year after they were married.

The only sadness in their lives was that Elizabeth could have no more children.

They however, found Ilesa enchanting.

All through her childhood she could not remember a time when the Vicarage was not filled with love and happiness.

It was only as her half-sister Doreen grew older that there was anything to disturb the atmosphere.

Being like her Mother, Doreen always wanted things she could not have.

It was a relief therefore when her grandfather the Earl, insisted on her going to a smart Seminary for Young Ladies in London.

She then went to what was known as a 'Finishing School' in Florence.

The two Schools certainly changed Doreen's life.

She had always found the Vicarage confining.

She was not interested in the villagers, or in anything that concerned her Father's vocation.

While the old Earl was alive, she spent most of her time at Harlestone Hall.

She loved the big rooms and high ceilings, and whenever possible she slept in one of the State Bedrooms with their huge four-poster beds.

"I like grandeur!" she said to her small half-sister, who did not understand what she meant.

Finally, when she was seventeen Doreen had 'come out' in London as a debutante.

She was presented at Buckingham Palace by one of the Earl's sisters, who had no daughters of her own.

At the end of her first Season Doreen had married Lord Barker.

It was considered an excellent match, despite the fact that he was very much older than she was.

From that moment, her Father, Stepmother and half-sister saw very little of her.

They did not miss her for the simple reason that she had always been somehow out of place in the Vicarage.

Elizabeth Harle had tried in every way to be a Mother to her stepdaughter.

But she knew privately that it was the one big failure in her life.

When two years ago she died Doreen had not even come back for the Funeral.

She did, however, send an enormous, if somewhat flamboyant, wreath.

It looked incongruous among the smaller but loving tributes that had been sent by the local people.

There were little bunches of flowers from the village children which Ilesa found very touching.

Because they all knew how much Elizabeth Harle had loved flowers, the whole neighbourhood had contributed.

They stripped their gardens of every leaf and blossom as a tribute to her.

To Mark Harle it was a blow that left him dazed.

He found it hard to believe that he had lost someone he had loved so dearly.

Ilesa understood, but there was little she could do to comfort him.

She only tried in every way she could to take her Mother's place.

She arranged the flowers in the Church, she visited the sick in the village and comforted the bereaved.

She also tried to find employment for the young people when they left School.

It had, the year before, come as a disaster to the whole village when the new Earl of Harlestone had closed the Big House.

It was not unreasonable because Robert had been appointed Governor of the North-West Frontier Province.

This meant he would be living in India for the next five years.

"It is no use, Mark," he had said to his brother, "I cannot afford to keep up the house as well as meet my expenses in India, which will be very heavy."

"What is to happen to the people who have always worked there?" Mark Harle had asked him. "Some of them have worked for us for over thirty years."

"I know, I know," his brother Robert said testily. "But I just cannot find the money!"

The two brothers had sat up talking all night.

Finally, on the Vicar's insistence, the Earl had agreed to retain four of the oldest servants to act as Caretakers.

Watkins the Head Gardener, Oakes, the Head Game-Keeper, were to keep their cottages.

"I am sure I can find local work for them to do," the Vicar said, "and I will help with their pensions, which will at least keep them from starving."

"You know you cannot afford to do that!" Robert protested. "The best thing we can do is to sell something."

His brother looked at him in consternation.

"Sell?" he enquired. "But everything in the house is entailed."

"There must be a few things that are not," Robert argued, "and there are some outlying plots of land that could be disposed of, even though we will not get much for them."

Finally, one way and another, the Earl found the means to allow Watkins and Oakes enough to live on.

The Vicar encouraged the gardener to grow fruit and vegetables that could be sold in the local market.

Oakes was to keep down the vermin and sell what rabbit, pigeons and ducks he could shoot or trap.

"It will not bring in much," Mark said to his brother, "but perhaps enough even to pay a youth to help them. At least it will keep them busy."

He gave a deep sigh as he added:

"I do not know what the village is going to do! As you well know, Robert, the great ambition of all the young people has always been to be taken on at the Big House."

"I know, I know!" Robert agreed. "But I can hardly refuse to become Governor of the North-West Frontier Province which is a great honour, simply because the village wants me to stay in England!"

What he said was meant to be a joke, but there was a bitter note in his voice.

17

"The real trouble," Mark said soothingly, "is that the Harles have never been rich, and Papa was extravagant, especially where horses were concerned."

"That is true," Robert agreed, "and I suggest you have the choice of two horses you most want, and I will sell the rest."

"Must you really do that?" the Vicar asked. "It seems a pity when there is such a very fine collection in the stables at the moment."

"I know, but I can hardly take them to India with me, and they will be a bit 'long in the tooth' when I get back!"

Finally the Vicar took four of the horses and the rest were sold.

Ilesa cried when she saw them being taken away.

She had always been allowed to ride any horses she liked in her grandfather's stables.

She had grown to love the animals and there was nothing she could not do with them.

"Miss Ilesa's got a way wi' 'orses," the grooms would say.

She was allowed to mount the most obstreperous and even those that were not fully broken.

She knew she had as they said, 'a way with' the animals.

The horses would obey her even though the stable-lads were too nervous to mount them.

The only good thing about shutting Harlestone Hall was that at least it was not leased to a stranger.

"If I were not still able to ride in the Park, swim

in the lake, and read the books in the Library," Ilesa said to her Father, "I would cry my eyes out!"

"I know that, my Dearest," the Vicar replied, "and that is why we must be very grateful that, if it is shut to everybody else, it is open to us."

There was no doubt however, that as the years passed they began to take their toll on the building.

The wooden doors and window-frames needed repainting.

The garden, with no one to tend it, began to look like a hay-field.

The flower-beds were disappearing amongst the weeds.

Ilesa had to fight her way through the nettles to pick the flowers which still managed to push their way through them.

Two of the green houses were in danger of falling in.

There did not seem to be any point in urging her Father to have them repaired.

"Your Uncle will be in India for at least another two years," he said.

Ilesa still went to the Library to get what books she wanted to read.

She would look at the pictures hanging on the walls and think how wonderful they would look if they were dusted.

The furniture wanted polishing, so did the fire places and the fire guard, as they had been before her grandfather had died.

One of the things however, that delighted Ilesa

was that he had left her Father in his Will two pictures.

They were not entailed, for he had been given them by his God-father.

They were two pictures by Stubbs.

As the Vicar pointed out, they had been cleverly framed to show them off to their best advantage.

"They are lovely, Papa," Ilesa exclaimed over and over again. "I am sure Grandpapa knew you would appreciate them more than anyone else."

"I am delighted to have them," the Vicar said, "and I am also exceedingly grateful to my Father for leaving me a little money which I can spend on those really in need."

Ilesa repressed an impulse to say that she was really in need of a new gown.

She knew her Father was thinking of those who could not get local employment now that the Big House was closed.

There were also the elderly.

They could no longer turn to His Lordship when their cottages needed repairing or they themselves were desperately in need of help.

Because he could never say no to anyone in need, the Vicar took on an extra man to look after the horses.

Also a boy he did not really need to work in the garden.

Mrs. Briggs, who had been at the Vicarage ever since Ilesa could remember, had help in the Kitchen.

Nanny, who took over the running of the house

very competently after Elizabeth Harle's death had had a young girl thrust upon her.

She proved to be more trouble than she was worth.

Nevertheless, if it was what the Master wanted, they accepted it all with a good grace.

Walking back to the Vicarage after leaving the Church, Ilesa was thinking of her Father's concern for two of the villagers who were seriously ill.

She was also planning to surprise him on his birthday which was the following week.

She had learned that a book had recently been published in London which contained illustrations of pictures by Stubbs.

She knew it would delight him to read it.

He would enjoy learning more about the Artist whose pictures now adorned his Study walls.

She decided that she would write and have the book sent to her.

She would give it to him on his birthday together with a number of other smaller presents.

All of which she would wrap up and tie with pink ribbon.

It was a custom her Mother had inaugurated not only at Christmastime, but also for birthdays.

"Everybody likes presents," she had said, "and the more, the merrier!"

She had always contrived to have at least half-a-dozen presents for Ilesa on her birthday.

The same number or even more for her husband.

They ranged from one large, fairly expensive present to something small and amusing.

A jar of the special mustard he preferred, a comb of honey, or a handkerchief embroidered with his initials.

Every present was a surprise, and fun to open.

Ilesa was determined that her Father should have the largest number of presents possible this year.

As she turned into the Vicarage drive, she stared in astonishment at a smart carriage drawn by two well-matched horses standing outside the front door.

She was certain as she drew nearer that the carriage was not one that belonged to any of their neighbours.

"Who can it be?" she wondered.

She tried to remember if her Father was at home.

Then she recalled that he had driven off early that morning.

He was visiting a Farmer on the outskirts of the Harlestone Estate whose wife was expecting a baby in two months.

"I hope to be back for luncheon," he had said to Ilesa before he left, "but if I am late, do not wait for me. You know how long-winded Farmer Johnson is!"

Ilesa had laughed.

She knew that because her Father was so sympathetic and understanding people were inclined to talk to him for far too long.

He knew however, that 'getting it off their chests', as he called it, was often a great help.

He was therefore patient and stayed when he visited people for far longer than he had intended.

"I wonder who it is who wants him?" Ilesa puzzled.

She reached the front door and had another quick look at the horses.

They were certainly outstanding.

She did not recognise the livery that the coachman on the box was wearing.

The front door was open and she went inside.

She entered the Drawing-Room which was on the other side of the house looking into the garden.

Standing by the window she saw a slender figure.

It was certainly somebody very smart, wearing a hat with feathers and an elegant bustle.

As she hesitated in the doorway, the woman turned round.

Ilesa gave a cry of pleasure.

"Doreen! I did not expect you! Where have you come from?"

She ran across the room to kiss her half-sister.

Doreen accepted the embrace, but made no attempt to return it.

"I found the house empty," she said. "Where were you?"

"I was arranging the flowers in the Church," Ilesa explained. "You know it is Saturday."

Doreen gave a little laugh which had no humour in it.

"Of course, it never occurred to me," she said, "and you certainly look somewhat untidy."

Ilesa pulled off her hat.

"I know," she said. "I went up to The Hall to pick some of the flowers there, but the place is so over-

23

grown that it is impossible not to be almost torn to bits by the briars."

"It is ridiculous to let it go to rack and ruin!" Doreen said sharply.

Ilesa knew it would be useles to try to explain that their Uncle could not afford to do anything else.

Instead she said:

"It is lovely to see you! Can I get you some coffee? Are you staying for luncheon?"

"I suppose so – if there is anything to eat!" Doreen replied.

"Of course there is," Ilesa answered, "and Mrs. Briggs will certainly do her best if she knows you are here."

"Good Heavens! Is that old woman still with you?" Doreen exclaimed.

"She looks older than she really is," Ilesa said quickly, "and we could not do without her. You know she has been with us ever since we were children."

Doreen's mind was obviously on something different.

After a moment she said:

"Well, go and tell Mrs. Briggs that I shall be here for luncheon. Then I want to talk to you."

"What about your coachman?" Ilesa asked.

Doreen hesitated for a moment. Then she said:

"He can eat here, if you can feed him. If not, he will have to go to the Inn."

"Of course he must have something to eat here!" Ilesa said.

She ran from the room.

In the Kitchen Mrs. Briggs was kneading the dough for their pudding tomorrow.

They always had a pie on Sunday because it was the Vicar's favourite.

"Mrs. Briggs," Ilesa said, raising her voice because the old woman was growing deaf, "Miss Doreen is here and is staying for luncheon."

"'Er Ladyship?" Mrs. Briggs exclaimed. "God bless my soul! She's not been 'ere for nigh three years!"

"I know that," Ilesa said, "but she is here now, and her coachman would like something to eat too. I am sure you can manage."

"Aye, Oi can manage right enough," Mrs. Briggs agreed, "an' it's lucky it is that I bought that leg o' lamb for luncheon today. It was to 'ave lasted most o' the week, but not wi' two extras gnawin' away at it!"

Mrs. Briggs was talking more to herself than to Ilesa who left her to hurry back to the Drawing-Room.

On the way she did her best to tidy her hair.

She knew she must look a mess compared to Doreen in her impeccable outfit.

Ilesa was wishing she had had time to put on one of her better gowns before her sister arrived.

Then she told herself philosophically that nothing she possessed could compare with what Doreen was wearing.

Doreen was now exceedingly rich since her elderly husband had died from a heart-attack three years ago.

Doreen had only come home once shortly after her bereavement.

Occasionally Ilesa and her Father had heard of what a success she was being in London.

They read in the social columns of the newspapers of parties she gave, attended by all the most important people in the Social World.

Their neighbours always talked about Doreen whenever Ilesa and her Father visited them.

"Your sister is one of the most beautiful women in London!" Ilesa had been told a hundred times. "I hear she is constantly at Marlborough House."

Although she lived in the country, Ilesa was aware what the ambition was of every woman.

It was to be invited to the house belonging to the Prince of Wales and his beautiful Danish wife, Princess Alexandra.

'The Marlborough House Set' was whispered about, gossiped about, and was an inevitable part of every conversation.

Ilesa felt sometimes she could write a book on all she had heard about it.

She was however not particularly interested.

She knew she was never likely to be invited there.

Her half-sister had never once invited her to stay with her in London.

Now, astoundingly, she had appeared without any warning.

Ilesa was wise enough to realise there would be some ulterior motive for Doreen's coming home.

It was such a strange thing for her to do that for a

moment she had been afraid that some tragedy had occurred.

Doreen however, certainly looked as if nothing could perturb her.

Ilesa did not miss the diamond and pearl ear-rings and the three strands of pearls at her throat.

There was a diamond brooch in the shape of a butterfly on the shoulder of her gown.

She could not help thinking that just one of Doreen's jewels could support a dozen people in the village.

It would make her Father very happy.

Then she told herself that her imagination was running away with her.

Doreen only communicated with her Father and herself at Christmas and ignored their birthdays.

Ilesa had been afraid that her Father would feel hurt.

Then she thought it over carefully.

From the moment Doreen had been sent to a smart School and then to Florence, she had made it more or less clear that she despised her family.

She had intimated that she wanted to live a very different sort of life.

It was certainly what she had achieved with Lord Barker.

Only occasionally did Ilesa think it was unkind.

Now that Doreen was a rich widow, she would not wish to spend time with her relatives in the country.

'I cannot think why she is here now!' Ilesa thought as she walked into the Drawing-Room.

While she was away, Doreen had made herself comfortable.

She had taken off her feathered hat and was lying back in an armchair with her feet on a footstool.

As Ilesa reached her she said:

"Now sit down and listen to what I have to tell you. You have to help me because there is no one else I can trust."

"Are you in . . some sort of trouble, Doreen?" Ilesa enquired.

"Of course I am!" Doreen snapped. "Otherwise, I would not be here."

"I am sorry," Ilesa said gently, "and of course Papa and I will help you if it is possible."

As she spoke she could not imagine how either of them could help Doreen in any way.

She could not be needing money: of that Ilesa was certain.

Because it seemed more friendly, she knelt down at her sister's feet and looked up at her.

"Now tell me, Doreen," she said softly, "what is worrying you."

Doreen gave a sigh that was really more one of exasperation than of distress.

"You have to help me," she said, "simply because there is no one else who can. What I want, needless to say, is very very important to me."

"What *do* you want?" Ilesa asked curiously.

"To put it bluntly," Doreen replied, "I want to marry the Duke of Mountheron."

Ilesa gave a little gasp.

28

"The Duke of Mountheron? But . . does he want to . . marry you?"

The questions seemed to tumble out of her mouth simply because she was so surprised.

She had somehow expected that sooner or later Doreen would marry again.

She felt sure it would be to someone just as important as Lord Barker had been and a brilliant match.

But even that was hardly on the same level as marrying a Duke!

As it happened, Ilesa had heard of the Duke of Mountheron because he had some outstanding race-horses.

Her Father who was an exceptionally good rider, took the '*Racing Times*' every week.

It always carried graphic descriptions of the horses that were running in every race that week, and went into details regarding their breeding.

There were also articles about their owners.

The Duke of Mountheron had won the Derby last year and his horse had come in second the year before.

He had in the last few years won nearly all the Classic races.

Ilesa and her Father had often discussed his stable.

"I hear he bought some mares from Syria," the Vicar said, "or it might have been his Father. Anyway, the horses have an Arab strain in them which makes them exceptional."

"I would love to see them!" Ilesa had exclaimed.

"So would I," the Vicar smiled, "and if there is

29

any chance of his having runners in any of the races near here, then of course we must try to attend."

He gave a sigh.

"Unfortunately Newmarket is too long a journey, and we would have to stay the night which would be expensive."

"If we left early, I dare say we could find our way back if there was a moon," Ilesa said.

The Vicar smiled.

"That is an idea, and we will certainly think about it. In the meantime, we have to decide which horses we are going to ride in the Point-to-Point next week. I am also hoping that *Red Rufus* will be strong enough for me to hunt with him next Autumn."

Red Rufus had hurt one of his legs and Ilesa was tending it.

She had bandaged it and massaged it.

The groom who looked after the horses was quite certain that she prayed every night for *Red Rufus* to get well.

Now she said:

"I assure you *Red Rufus* will be perfectly well in a month's time. He will have to be ridden carefully at first, but I am certain he will be well enough to hunt in the Autumn."

The Vicar patted her arm.

"That is what I want to do, and I know, Dearest child, it is due to you that he is not completely crippled."

He smiled again.

"In Mediaeval times you would have been burned as a Witch, so just be careful!"

"If I am a Witch, then I am like Mama, who was a White one," Ilesa replied. "You know that is what they used to say about her in the village. They never sent for the Doctor, but always for Mama. Her herbs healed them far quicker than anything the Doctor could prescribe."

"That is true," the Vicar agreed, "and when I had a headache, she used to massage my forehead and it disappeared immediately."

Ilesa did not answer.

The pain in her Father's voice when he spoke of the wife he had loved and lost was very poignant.

She knew there was nothing she could say to comfort him.

Now she looked at her half-sister in surprise.

It flashed through her mind that only her Mother would have been able to cope with a difficult situation like Doreen wanting to marry a Duke.

There was a little pause. Then Doreen said:

"I *must* marry him! I *will* marry him! I am *determined* to marry him! But at this moment only you and Papa can help me!"

CHAPTER TWO

Ilesa was just going to answer when there was a barking and scratching at the door.

She jumped up.

"It is the dogs," she said unnecessarily. "They have been shut up while I was in the Church. Now they know I am back."

"Do not let them come near me!" Doreen said sharply. "They will leave hairs on my skirt."

Ilesa was not listening.

She hurried across the room to open the door.

The dogs burst in, jumping and barking with delight at seeing her.

They were two Spaniels and they went everywhere with her.

If she was away, even for an hour or so, they behaved as if she had come back from a long voyage.

She patted them and calmed them down.

Then she sat down again on the floor beside her sister.

"I am sorry, Doreen," she said. "I know you dislike dogs, but they will be no trouble now."

The dogs had in fact settled down near Ilesa and were no longer making a noise.

Doreen did not speak and after a moment Ilesa said gently:

"You were saying that you needed us to help you."

She heard her sister take a deep breath before she began:

"I met the Duke two months ago, and I knew at once he was bowled over by my beauty."

There was a note of satisfaction in her voice which Ilesa did not miss.

"He is of course very sought after in London," Doreen went on, "and that he attaches himself to me at parties, and hostesses seat us next to each other at dinners, is very flattering."

"I can understand his being bowled over by your beauty," Ilesa said. "You are much more beautiful now than you have ever been, Doreen."

"I know that," her sister replied, "but as you know, I am nearly twenty-six, and I want to be married again."

"I am sure lots of men have already asked you to be their wife," Ilesa said loyally.

"That is true," Doreen agreed. "At the same time, the Duke of Mountheron is unique and, as I have already said, I intend to marry him."

There was a pause.

Then Ilesa said, almost as if she was speaking to herself:

"But . . he has . . not yet . . asked you?"

"He has been very near to doing so," Doreen

replied. "In fact, the last time we were together, I felt instinctively that the words were trembling on his lips."

She gave a little sigh and Ilesa asked:

"Then what . . happened?"

"That is what I am going to tell you," Doreen said in a different voice. "The Duke had to leave London for a short-time, and because I was lonely I went out with Lord Randall, who fell in love with me more than two years ago."

Ilesa was listening attentively, realising that somebody else had come on the scene.

"He persuaded me, against my better judgement," Doreen continued, "to stay with him last night at an Hotel called '*The Three Feathers*', which is about ten miles from here."

Ilesa stared at her sister in astonishment.

"Stay . . with . . you?" she questioned. "Alone?"

"Oh, do not be so ridiculous, Ilesa!" Doreen said crossly. "You may live here among the turnips and cabbages, but you must be aware that in London every pretty married woman has *affaires de coeur*. As I have said, Hugo Randall has been in love with me for some time."

"But . . you are in . . love with . . the Duke!"

Ilesa was so surprised and shocked that she found the words difficult to utter and they were almost incoherent.

There was a little pause before Doreen answered:

"I intend to *marry* the Duke, which is a very different thing."

Ilesa felt bewildered.

She had vaguely known, as Doreen had said, that people in London especially those in the Marlborough House Set, had fairly promiscuous love-affairs.

These were talked about *sotto voce* by some of the people at parties she had attended with her Father and Mother.

Somehow she had never thought of any of her own friends or relations being so involved.

It was an incredible shock to learn that her sister, who was in love with one man, should have an *affaire de coeur* with another.

She could not understand it.

She could not accept it as something happening in her own experience.

Her Father and Mother had been so completely devoted to each other.

They had never discussed or gossiped about such matters.

"What happened," Doreen was saying, "and you can hardly believe I could have such bad luck, was that at dawn this morning, when I was asleep, a man whom I know, and whose name is Sir Mortimer Jackson, burst into my bedroom!

"'The Hotel is on fire!' he shouted. 'Get up quickly or you will be burnt to death!'"

Ilesa gave a little cry of horror.

"The Hotel was on fire, Doreen? How terrible! How did you escape?"

"As it turned out, it was a false alarm," Doreen replied, "but of course I was extremely frightened."

"Naturally," Ilesa murmured.

"Hugo Randall got up . ." Doreen continued.

". . . From . . your . . bed?" Ilesa stammered.

"Yes, yes, from my bed!" Doreen said, testily. "He would have gone back to his own room in just a few minutes. That is why it was such bad luck that ghastly Sir Mortimer should burst in on us!"

She spoke very angrily, and there was a frown between her beautiful eyes.

"And you . . say there was . . not really . . a fire?" Ilesa murmured.

"Hugo Randall went to see what all the fuss was about and found that one of the servants had upset some hot fat, or something on the stove."

Doreen's voice was seething as she continued:

"It caused a dense cloud of smoke to rise up past Sir Mortimer's window. I always thought he was a stupid, idiotic man, but unfortunately he is also dangerous!"

"You . . mean," Ilesa said, trying to understand, "he recognised you."

"Of course he did," Doreen said, "and because I have always disliked him, and made my feelings very clear, he will undoubtedly tell the Duke what he saw."

At last Ilesa understood the problem and why Doreen was so upset.

If the Duke learned of the way she had behaved with Lord Randall, he was not likely to ask her to become his wife.

She looked at her sister helplessly.

How could she possibly help her to get out of such a predicament?

"I have thought it out carefully," Doreen said in a

practical manner. "What I have to do is to make the Duke propose to me before he returns to London where Sir Mortimer will be waiting for him."

"Are you . . are you quite . . certain that is . . what he . . will . . do?" Ilesa asked. "It sounds very ungentlemanly. Papa has always said . . that a Gentleman never mentions a woman's name . . disparagingly in . . public, or he would be thrown out of his Clubs."

"Men like Sir Mortimer do not behave like Gentlemen!" Doreen said scathingly. "He ingratiates himself with the nobility by giving them information which they find amusing, or else in some way helpful."

"Then how can you prevent him from telling the Duke about you?" Ilesa asked.

"I am making sure," Doreen replied, "as I have just said, that I see the Duke first. That is why I sent a note immediately by my footman asking him to come here this afternoon."

Ilesa stared at her in sheer astonishment.

"To come here?" she repeated, "but why? And how? Where is he?"

Doreen was about to answer. Then she gave an exclamation.

"The servants!" she cried. "I never thought of the servants!"

She jumped out of the chair in which she had been sitting and Ilesa heard her running across the hall to the front door.

She supposed that Mrs. Briggs would not invite the coachman in for luncheon until it was ready.

He would therefore be with the carriage waiting for instructions outside the front door.

She could hear Doreen's voice in the distance although she could not hear what she was saying.

There came the sound of rolling wheels.

She knew that the carriage was being turned round.

She did not move, but one of the Spaniels curled up beside her and she stroked its head.

She found it hard to believe what her Sister had told her, and even harder to understand her behaviour.

How was it possible that Doreen could go to an Inn and share a bed with a man to whom she was not married?

Ilesa had never been to *The Three Feathers* but she had heard it was thought to be the best in the County.

In fact it was used by Gentlemen from London when they took part in the local Point-to-Points or Steeple-Chases.

Vaguely at the back of her mind, she remembered her grandfather recommending friends to stay there for the Hunt Ball or some other important function when The Hall was full.

People from London then had to be accommodated wherever they could find a bed.

But Ilesa had never imagined that her own sister would stay there.

Much less behave in a manner which would have horrified her Mother and would deeply distress her Father.

Doreen came back into the room.

"It slipped my mind," she said as she walked towards the chair in which she had been sitting, "that if the Duke comes here, his servants will talk to my Coachman. He might tell them where I was staying last night."

"But . . but how do . . you know the Duke . . will come . . here?" Ilesa asked.

"I remembered," Doreen explained, "that Papa has those pictures by Stubbs, which you both made such a fuss about."

Ilesa looked at her sister questioningly and Doreen went on:

"The Duke has a special collection of Stubbs' pictures."

She gave a little sigh of satisfaction.

"It suddenly occurred to me that as he was staying in the neighbourhood, he would be thrilled to see Papa's pictures, and of course I shall be here waiting for him."

"You say he is in the neighbourhood?" Ilesa asked. "Where is he staying?"

"With the Lord Lieutenant, of course, the Marquess of Exford!"

Doreen spoke as if her sister had asked a silly question, and Ilesa knew she was right.

Of course the Duke of Mountheron would be staying with the Marquess of Exford.

He was a very distinguished man with a notably fine stable.

His house was some distance from Littlestone, but

the Vicar and his wife had often been invited to dine.

They also went to the Garden Party which the Marquess and his wife gave every year.

"If the Duke is staying with the Lord Lieutenant," Ilesa said reflectively, "do you really think he will come here because you have asked him to?"

"I have told you, it is only a question of time before he asks me to marry him," Doreen snapped, "and I cannot risk losing everything by letting that rat Sir Mortimer blacken my character!"

Ilesa thought for a moment. Then she said:

"What will you do if he tells the Duke after he has proposed to you?"

"That is where you have to help me," Doreen said. "I stayed here last night. In fact, I have been here ever since the Duke left London, which was two days ago."

Ilesa stared at her sister.

"You mean . . you are going to . . tell him a . . complete lie?"

"Of course," Doreen admitted, "and you are going to substantiate it and make it very clear that I have been staying in my old home, enjoying myself by being with you and Papa."

Ilesa drew in her breath.

"You know . . Papa will not . . lie," she said quickly.

"Then we will talk to him about it very carefully, and you must say to the Duke:

"'It has been lovely to have Doreen here these last few days!'"

It was with difficulty that Ilesa did not reply that she too disliked telling lies.

Her Father and Mother had been very insistent that she should always tell the truth, the whole truth and nothing but the truth.

Yet she knew now she had to do what Doreen wished.

Otherwise her sister would get into one of her tantrums, which had always frightened her when she was a child.

Because she was so much younger and smaller Doreen had bullied her.

She had made Ilesa do what she wanted, even if it meant pulling her hair or slapping her.

Ilesa doubted if she would use actual violence.

But she was well aware what a scene there would be if she told Doreen that she would not support her by telling lies.

Doreen characteristically assumed that Ilesa had acquiesced in doing what she wanted.

"Now we have not much time," she said briskly, "so you had better go and tidy yourself. I have no wish for the Duke to think that my sister is a country-bumpkin!"

Ilesa felt the colour come into her cheeks.

It had always been the same.

Whenever she was with Doreen, she was always made to feel awkward and out of place, and definitely inferior.

"I will put on the best dress I have," she said, getting to her feet. "At the same time, Doreen, as you are well aware, there has been very little money to spend on clothes. Papa has to help the people who have been unemployed ever since Uncle Robert shut The Hall."

"If you had any sense," Doreen retorted, "you would not allow Papa to throw his money away on a lot of ne'er-do-wells!"

She rose to her feet adding:

"I had better come upstairs with you and see how I can make you look at least decent!"

"I think," Ilesa said in a small voice, "we had better have luncheon first. It looks as if Papa will not be back in time. It will be ready by now, and Mrs. Briggs will be upset if we let it get cold."

"Oh, very well," Doreen said with a bad grace, "and for goodness' sake, see if there is something decent to eat in the house in case, although I think it is unlikely, the Duke stays for dinner."

Ilesa's eyes widened.

She knew this without any warning, would be a catastrophe.

It was then old Briggs, who acted as Butler, opened the door.

He had been at the Vicarage for as long as his wife.

He had however, never been a Butler in the proper sense of the word.

But because he loved his master and his mistress, when she had been alive, he had done his best.

Now, like Nanny, he was almost one of the family.

"Luncheon be ready, Miss Ilesa," he announced, "an' Mrs. Briggs says she's done 'er best, but she can't do no miracles at a moment's notice, an' that's the truth!"

Doreen did not speak and Ilesa said:

"I am sure Mrs. Briggs has worked miracles, as she always does!"

Briggs smiled at her before he hobbled, rather than walked, because he had rheumatism, down the passage to the Dining-Room.

Doreen moved elegantly across the room.

"We need not waste much time in eating, when we have so much else to do," she said.

Ilesa did not answer.

She was thinking how disappointed Mrs. Briggs would be if Doreen did not say something nice to her when luncheon was finished.

They walked into the Dining-Room.

It was a very pretty room and, as in the Drawing-Room, the windows overlooked the garden.

The silver on the table shone in the sunlight.

If there was one thing Briggs enjoyed, it was cleaning the silver.

He also carved the lamb as well as the Vicar might have done.

When he served it Ilesa thought it was so well cooked that it would be difficult for Doreen to find fault.

All the same, luncheon was an uncomfortable meal with Doreen saying very little.

Ilesa was feeling nervous about what was going to happen.

She was wondering, if the Duke did arrive, as

Doreen was so confident he would, how she could leave them alone without it appearing contrived.

It might be embarrassing if the Duke guessed what was expected of him.

Ilesa knew very little about men.

Yet she was sure a man like the Duke would resent being pressurised into doing anything he did not want to do.

In fact he might very well manage to avoid being put in a compromising situation.

In which case Doreen would obviously be extremely angry and complain it was all her fault.

When they had finished the lamb, which was tender, and the new potatoes which went with it, there was a dish of strawberries.

Fortunately Ilesa had picked them only yesterday in the overgrown Kitchen-garden at The Hall.

She knew that Mrs. Briggs had been keeping them as a treat for her Father.

They were served at luncheon with a junket she had made originally just for Ilesa.

Doreen refused both dishes.

"I do not like strawberries," she said, "and as for junket, I have not seen it since I left the Nursery!"

Because it was possible that what she said might be heard in the Kitchen, Ilesa felt embarrassed.

She gave a warning glance at her sister as she said:

"I am sure you remember that Mrs. Briggs's junket is quite different from anyone else's, and we always think of it as a speciality of the Vicarage."

"Oh, very well!" Doreen said.

She took a spoonful and looked at it disdainfully before she tasted it.

Then, because it was impossible to find fault she ate quite a large helping.

Then there was coffee, after which the two sisters went upstairs to Ilesa's bedroom.

Without waiting for Ilesa to do so, Doreen pulled open the wardrobe door.

There were not many gowns hanging there.

Ilesa knew all too well that most of them were well-worn, and one or two were becoming threadbare.

"Surely you have something better than these?" Doreen asked.

"I . . I am afraid . . not," Ilesa answered. "I was going to ask Papa to give me a new gown, but there have been so . . many other things to . . do."

She hesitated over the last words.

The truth was that her Father spent all the money he had on other people.

"Then I suppose I shall have to lend you something."

Ilesa looked at her half-sister in surprise.

"I thought you had sent your carriage away?"

"I am not half-witted," Doreen answered. "I told my Coachman to leave my luggage, which I had taken with me for the night, at the back door. I suppose you have somebody who can carry it upstairs?"

"I will go and tell Briggs to get one of the gardeners to do it," Ilesa said. "As you can see, he is too old, and his rheumatism is too bad for him to carry anything heavy."

Doreen did not answer.

Ilesa ran from the room and down the back stairs.

She found Briggs in the Kitchen and told him what she wanted.

"Are yer sayin'," Mrs. Briggs asked, "that 'Er Ladyship's stayin' 'ere t'night?"

"I am not sure," Ilesa answered.

It suddenly struck her that her sister would try to make the Duke take her with him to wherever he intended to go.

Doreen had not said so, but she had sent away her carriage.

There would be no way for her to leave the Vicarage unless the Duke conveyed her in his own carriage.

"Doreen is clever!" she told herself. "I would . . never have thought of . . that!"

It was some time before Doreen's very expensive leather trunk was brought up to her bedroom.

After the gardeners had set it down and left them alone, Ilesa undid the straps.

Doreen simply sat in a chair giving instructions.

"There is a gown I packed at the last minute," she said, "just in case I stayed for two nights at *The Three Feathers*. It is pale blue with a little muslin collar."

Ilesa found the gown.

It was exceedingly pretty, but she thought far too grand to wear at an Inn or, for that matter, in the country.

46

However Doreen said:

"I suppose I shall have to give it to you."

"Oh, you . . cannot do . . that!" Ilesa cried. "I am sure you will want to keep anything so beautiful."

"I have always thought it did not suit me particularly well, and was not really smart enough. But it is certainly an improvement on anything you possess."

"Thank you . . thank you . . very much!" Ilesa said. "It is a . . beautiful gown, and I am . . thrilled to have it."

She put it on while her sister sat criticising her appearance.

"Why can you not do your hair in a more fashionable manner?" she enquired. "The way you do it now went out at least five years ago!"

Ilesa smiled.

"There are not many people in Littlestone who know what the fashion is," she said. "While the dogs and horses with whom I spend most of my time are not really very particular."

Doreen was not amused.

"You must think of your position," she said, "for after all you are my sister!"

"Yes . . of course," Ilesa said, "but we have not seen anything of you lately."

"I am such a sensation in London," Doreen explained, "that I really have no time to go anywhere else!"

Then as if she could not resist being boastful, she started to describe to Ilesa exactly what a success she was.

She also told her how many men had laid their hearts at her feet.

Ignorant of the Social World as Ilesa was, she realised that a great number of the men who paid Doreen such extravagant compliments were already married.

Because she read the Racing newspapers, she knew a number of Doreen's admirers were race-horse owners.

Her sister talked and went on talking.

Ilesa tried to tell herself that she must not judge Doreen by the same standards and the same principles as her Father upheld in Littlestone.

'Hers is a different world,' she thought, 'so different, that I must not be stupid enough to compare the two.'

She was aware that it was only because she was in trouble that Doreen had come home.

She had known for a long time that Doreen had no affection for her family.

Unless she had needed Ilesa's help, it would never have occurred to her to visit the Vicarage.

"Now be very, very careful what you say," Doreen warned her when they got back to the problem of the Duke. "Convince him that I have been here for two nights and I have seen no one except you and Papa. We have just sat here in the evening, talking over old times."

"And you really think His Grace will believe that," Ilesa asked, "if later Sir Mortimer tells him that he definitely saw you with Lord Randall at *The Three Feathers*?"

"It was very early in the morning, and although Hugo had unfortunately pulled back the curtains," Doreen said, "Sir Mortimer was in a very agitated state. If he saw somebody who in a little way resembled me, he was obviously mistaken."

She paused for a moment before she went on:

"A naked woman with fair hair falling over her shoulders might be anyone, and if I insist that I was not there, and you confirm that I was here, why should the Duke believe Sir Mortimer?"

She sounded very confident.

But Ilesa knew perceptively that she was in fact nervous and on edge.

She could understand that it had been a terrible shock for Doreen when Sir Mortimer had burst into her bedroom.

Then when she learnt it was only a false alarm, it had been infuriating to know that she was in the hands of a man she both disliked and distrusted.

With Ilesa looking very unlike her usual self, the two sisters went downstairs.

There was still no sign of the Vicar.

Doreen, determined to make certain there was no possibility of there being any mistakes, said:

"You must tell Papa, if he comes home after the Duke has arrived, that I have come back to see you because I felt guilty at having been away for too long, and I do not wish the Duke or anyone else to know how long it has been."

"I am sure Papa would not be so tactless as to reproach you in front of a stranger," Ilesa replied.

"Well, just tell him that I am thrilled to be back,

and that it would be a mistake for anyone in London to think I was heartless or ashamed of my family."

Ilesa did not answer, and Doreen said in a disagreeable tone of voice:

"It is extremely annoying to think The Hall is not open! I could have taken the Duke there, and I am sure he would have been extremely impressed by the way it looked in Grandpapa's day."

"It is very different now," Ilesa said with a sigh. "There is dust everywhere, soot has fallen down the chimneys, and the windows are so dirty that they make the rooms dark in the daytime."

"I do not want to hear about it," Doreen retorted. "I just think it is most tiresome that Uncle Robert should have rushed off to India and left the place in such a mess."

Ilesa knew that she was longing to show the Duke that her family had a large house and a big estate.

She thought privately that the Duke would hardly be impressed anyway.

From all she had read about him, he had a great number of possessions.

He was doubtless in consequence very conceited.

She felt he would spoil the happy atmosphere of her home, and it was a mistake for him to come here.

"He belongs to London," she told herself, "with women like Doreen, who are very beautiful but who do things that would have shocked Mama, and in fact, shock me!"

The hours were passing.

Now she was aware that Doreen was tense and listening for every sound.

To Ilesa it was a relief that it seemed the Duke was not going to appear.

But in that case Doreen would be frantic at the idea of Sir Mortimer contacting him and making trouble before she could see the Duke.

Ilesa was telling herself it was now definitely too late for the Duke to arrive, when there was a 'rat-tat' on the front door.

If it had been her Father, he would have walked straight in.

Since it was not her Father, it must be the Duke.

Doreen thought the same.

She rose from her chair to stand in front of the fireplace.

While Ilesa was changing, Doreen had spent a great deal of time rearranging her hair and powdering her face.

She looked lovely – there was no doubt about that.

In fact, her beauty seemed to outshine the small Drawing-Room, and it was obvious she belonged to another world.

The door opened.

"'Is Grace the Duke o' Mountheron, M'Lady!" old Briggs announced in a loud voice.

CHAPTER THREE

The Duke of Mountheron was having breakfast with his host and hostess the Marquess and Marchioness of Exford.

He and his host had been riding since seven o'clock and he had much enjoyed the exercise.

He had ridden one of the Marquess's most spirited and well-bred horses.

They were discussing what they would do in the morning, when a servant came in with a note on a silver salver.

He offered it to the Duke who took it with surprise.

He immediately recognised the hand-writing and read it quickly.

Then he said to the Marchioness:

"This is a letter from Lady Barker. I had no idea that her home was in this vicinity, and that her Father is a Vicar."

"He is indeed," the Marchioness replied "and a very charming and delightful man."

"She tells me," the Duke went on, as if he found it hard to believe, "that her Father has two excellent pictures by Stubbs which she thinks I would like to see."

"They are certainly some of his best work," the Marquess confirmed, "and Mark Harle was fortunate that his Father was able to leave them to him, as they were not entailed."

The Duke raised his eye-brows and the Marquess explained:

"I should have thought you would have known that the beautiful Lady Barker's grandfather was the Earl of Harlestone, and her Father a younger son."

"I had no idea," the Duke said.

He paused reflectively before he added:

"I have met the present Earl. Has he not gone to India?"

"He has been appointed Governor of the North-West Frontier Province," the Marquess said. "While it was undoubtedly an honour for him, it has been a tragedy for the neighbourhood!"

"Why is that?" the Duke enquired.

"Because," the Marquess explained, "Robert Harle shut up the family house and dismissed practically all the people who worked for him. It has worried his brother, the Vicar, a great deal."

He gave a short laugh before he continued:

"He talked me into taking on two grooms I do not need and an extra game-keeper!"

The Marchioness smiled.

"No one can resist the Vicar when he is pleading! I now have two young housemaids I do not really require."

She paused for a moment to add:

"Mark Harle's second daughter, Ilesa, is the most delightful girl and has been trying to take her Mother's place in the village. She looks after women who are ill and the young who cannot find employment now that The Hall is closed."

"As bad as that?" the Duke enquired.

"Worse," the Marchioness answered, "for as you well know, in a small village the owner of the Big House is almost the only employer."

The Duke nodded and the Marchioness continued:

"The distress caused by Robert Harle's going to India is breaking his brother's heart and also, I think, that of Mark's daughter."

The Duke looked down again at the note he held in his hand.

"Lady Barker has invited me to call and see her Father's pictures on my way home."

"Then it is certainly something you should do," the Marquess agreed, "except, of course, that you will want to add them to your own collection."

"I have a feeling," the Marchioness joined in, "that the Vicar enjoys his pictures as much as His Grace enjoys his, and would not part with them for a King's ransom!"

"Then I will be very tactful and will not ask him to sell them!" the Duke replied.

He was curious about the Stubbs' pictures.

He had been buying for some time every one which came up for sale and he had, he knew, one of the best collections in England.

. . . .

Later in the afternoon the Duke drove in his travelling-carriage drawn by four horses towards Littlestone village.

He was surprised that Doreen Barker had always talked about her husband and his possessions, but never about her family.

He thought a little cynically that perhaps she was not particularly proud of being a Vicar's daughter, even if he was the younger son of an Earl.

She was certainly very beautiful, and her beauty had taken London by storm.

The Duke, however, was well aware that she had pursued him rather than he, her.

He had in fact, allowed himself to submit to the obvious invitation in her very expressive eyes.

He would not have been the connoisseur he was of women if he had not appreciated the perfection of her figure, and her classical features.

It would certainly be something new to see her in the country.

He wondered what her Father, being a Vicar, thought of her somewhat outrageous behaviour in London.

The Duke was well aware he was not Doreen's first lover.

Nor, he thought with a twist of his lips, would he be her last.

At the same time, she was undeniably the most beautiful woman in Mayfair.

As the Duke walked into the Drawing-Room after Brigg's announcement, Ilesa held her breath.

She was anxious to see this man whom her sister intended to marry.

She was sure she would not like him.

She strongly disapproved of the way he and her sister were behaving.

Moreover, if as she suspected, it was the Duke's habit to have *affaires de coeur* with every beautiful woman he met, she despised him.

"It is very wrong, and Doreen should be aware of it!" she told herself.

Then as she looked at the Duke, she was surprised.

He was not in the least what she had expected.

He was tall, broad-shouldered and extremely handsome.

There was something quite different about him from the picture she had formed in her mind.

As he walked into the room, she seemed to feel his vibrations from the moment he appeared.

Then as the dogs jumped up excitedly and ran towards him he bent down to pat first one spaniel, then the other.

It was an action that seemed to make him more human.

Certainly more understanding than the rather intimidating Nobleman of her imagination whom Doreen wished to marry because of his title.

Her sister moved forward.

"Drogo!" she exclaimed in a cooing voice that Ilesa had not heard before. "How wonderful of you to come! I was praying that you would have the time to come and see me before you went on to Heron."

"How could I refuse such a delightful invitation as to see your Father's pictures?" the Duke replied.

Doreen was now standing very near to him, looking up at him.

Both her hands were in his, and he raised one to his lips.

"Need I say that you are looking very beautiful?" he asked.

"That is what I want to hear," Doreen replied softly.

The Duke looked towards Ilesa.

In a different tone of voice Doreen said:

"Let me introduce my sister Ilesa."

"Doreen never told me," the Duke said, holding out his hand, "that she had a sister."

Ilesa smiled.

"I have of course, heard about your horses, Your Grace," she said. "Are they really as fine as the newspapers say they are?"

The Duke's eyes twinkled.

"Better!" he asserted.

"Then you are very, very lucky, or perhaps very clever!" Ilesa remarked.

"I think that is a somewhat roundabout compliment which I appreciate," the Duke laughed.

The spaniels had sat down when they started talking.

Now they raised their heads.

They told Ilesa that her Father had returned.

"I think that is Papa," she said quickly to Doreen.

With a warning glance she ran across the room and let herself out into the hall.

She was right.

The Vicar was just coming in through the front door.

As soon as he saw his daughter he asked:

"Who is here? That is an exceedingly fine team of horses outside!"

"They belong to the Duke of Mountheron, Papa," Ilesa replied, "but before you meet him, I want to speak to you alone for a moment."

The Vicar seemed surprised, but he put his hat down on one of the chairs and walked towards his Study.

Ilesa followed him, and when they were both inside she shut the door.

"Now, what is all this about?" the Vicar asked, "and why should Mountheron, of all people, want to see me?"

"He has come to see Doreen," Ilesa explained.

"Doreen?" the Vicar exclaimed. "Do you mean – she is here?"

"She arrived unexpectedly just before luncheon," Ilesa said, "and, Papa, it is very, very important that when you go into the Drawing-Room you do not seem surprised to see her, because she is supposed to have been here since the day before yesterday."

"I do not know what all this is about," the Vicar said.

"I know it is complicated, Papa," Ilesa said, "but please, it is very important that you should pretend that she has stayed here for the last two nights."

"I do not understand what is going on," her Father

said sharply, "but I am not telling lies for Doreen, or for anyone else."

"It is not exactly a question of lies," Ilesa said slowly.

Then she had an idea.

"You see, Papa," she said, "Doreen is in love with the Duke, and she thinks he is about to propose to her. But she does not want him to think that she is running after him."

To her relief the Vicar smiled.

"That is sensible, at any rate," he said. "A man likes to do his own hunting."

"I was sure you would understand, Papa, and please treat Doreen as if you had seen her here at dinner the last two nights! Then we can leave her to capture the Duke in her own way . ."

The Vicar laughed.

"She will be very clever if she can do that!" he said. "I am quite certain that Mountheron has been pursued by ambitious women ever since he left School, and Doreen will find it hard to lead him to the altar."

"She longs to be a Duchess," Ilesa said.

"I suppose that is the ambition of a lot of women, except for someone like your Mother and, I hope, you!"

Ilesa smiled at him.

"The only thing I want, Papa is, when I marry, to be as happy as you and Mama were."

"And that is what I want for you," the Vicar replied.

At the same time, Ilesa saw the pain in his eyes which was always there when he spoke of his wife.

Then he said:

"Now you have told me how I am to behave, let us go and meet the Duke!"

He walked from the Study and Ilesa followed him.

When they went into the Drawing-Room Ilesa was aware that her sister was tense and afraid of what her Father might say.

The Vicar however was entirely at his ease.

"This is a surprise!" he said as he walked towards the Duke holding out his hand. "I could not imagine as I arrived home who of all my Parishioners would have the finest team of horses I have ever seen!"

The Duke laughed.

"I am glad you admire them! They are a new acquisition and have been so well broken in that it is a delight to drive them."

The Vicar walked towards the fireplace and stood with his back to it.

"I must congratulate you," he said, "on your success in the Grand National. It is a pity you were 'pipped at the post', but your horse certainly did its best."

"That is what I thought," the Duke agreed, "and talking of horses, Vicar, I suspect your daughter has told you why I was so anxious to visit you."

The Vicar looked at him enquiringly, and Ilesa knew that he thought the Duke was about to say that he wished to marry Doreen.

Instead the Duke explained:

"I have been told that you possess two fine paintings by Stubbs. As you may know, I have a collection of which I am very proud."

"I have heard that," the Vicar said, "and I understand that you bought a particularly fine painting of his at Christie's last month."

"That is true," the Duke agreed, "but I am very anxious to see yours."

The Vicar made a gesture with his hand.

"Then of course, I am only too willing to show Your Grace my Stubbs', interesting but too few to be called a collection."

He walked across the room to lead the way to the door and Doreen flashed a glance at her sister.

Ilesa knew that she was extremely relieved.

Her Father had ignored her, making it obvious that he took her presence for granted.

The Vicar led the way back to the Study where he had been a few minutes before with Ilesa.

Hanging on one wall, so that it had the light from the window to show it at its best, was a picture.

Ilesa knew it was one of the most controversial and unusual of Stubbs' masterpieces.

As soon as the Duke looked at it he gave what was almost a cry of delight.

"You have the portrait of John Musters!" he exclaimed. "I have always wanted to see it!"

"I thought it would interest you," the Vicar said.

Ilesa knew the story of it, which she had heard a hundred times from the moment her Father had acquired it.

John Musters had been painted by Stubbs with his wife Sophia.

Unfortunately a very unhappy relationship developed between them and he believed she had been unfaithful to him.

He therefore insisted on her being painted out of the picture and replaced by the Reverend Philip Story.

Stubbs had done what he was asked to do by obliterating Sophia's figure and substituting the Vicar.

But he omitted to convert the side-saddle on which Sophia had been seated into one appropriate to a man.

The Vicar made sure that the Duke realised this, and said laughingly:

"Of course it is a sensible thing for me to have a picture of the Vicar, although I cannot rival his achievement of having fourteen children!"

The Duke laughed.

"I should hope not! But he evidently shared John Muster's passion for fox-hunting. Munster had a famous pack of hounds."

"We have said everything that can be said about this picture," the Vicar said. "Now look at the other one."

The second picture the Vicar had inherited from his Father was on another wall.

It portrayed a number of individual hounds, arranged across the picture as if they were posed for a judge's eye – dog, bitch, dog, bitch, dog.

The Duke stood looking at it for some time.

"This is the only known work, Vicar," he said, "in which Stubbs arranged hounds in such a manner.

You are extremely lucky to have it, and I am very envious."

"I am sure there is no need for Your Grace to be that," the Vicar said, "when you yourself, have so many examples of Stubbs' work."

"Which of course you must see," the Duke said. "When can you come to stay with me at Heron and tell me what I do not know about my own pictures?"

The Vicar laughed.

"I should have to be very clever to do that, but of course it would give me great pleasure to see not only your Stubbs' but also your horses."

The Duke hesitated a moment. Then he said:

"I was on my way home today, but if you could be good enough to offer me a bed for the night, we could all go to Heron tomorrow."

The Vicar looked surprised.

Then before he could speak, Doreen exclaimed:

"That is a wonderful idea! I would love, Papa to see Heron, which is the most beautiful house I have ever known."

The way she spoke made it very clear that she also appreciated its owner.

Then as she realised that the Duke was looking at Ilesa, she said quickly:

"I am sure it would be difficult however for my sister to come. She has so many duties here in the village."

"The duties of both of us, as far as that is concerned," the Vicar said, "will be finished after Matins tomorrow morning. I have no Sunday Evening Service."

This was true.

The village was so depleted since the Big House had been closed that it was possible for the villagers who were left to make up only one congregation on a Sunday.

The Vicar had therefore for the time being discontinued Evensong.

Only with Ilesa he read the Service in the privacy of his own Study.

"In which case," the Duke said, "it will give me great pleasure to invite you and both your daughters to Heron."

If he was to stay the night, that meant he would be there also for dinner.

Ilesa slipped away to tell Mrs. Briggs that they had an extra guest as well as Doreen.

Mrs. Briggs held up her hands in horror.

At the same time Ilesa knew she was really delighted to have the opportunity of cooking for a Duke.

She would be determined to do her best.

Briggs was resting his bad legs on a stool.

"I think," Ilesa said to him, "we have a bottle of claret which His Lordship gave Papa before he went to India."

"Tha's roight, Miss Ilesa," Briggs agreed, "an' there be some white wine too 'Is Lordship brings down from t'Hall, not as much as we'd like, but 'nough fer 'Is Grace."

"I know I can leave it to you, Briggs," Ilesa said.

As she left the Kitchen she was well aware that her sister had no wish for her to go to Heron.

She had seen the expression on Doreen's face when the Duke had invited them all.

It seemed ridiculous that a woman as beautiful as Doreen should be jealous of anyone.

"I must be very careful," she told herself. "Anyway, why should he even notice me when Doreen is looking so lovely?"

At the same time she knew that she herself was vividly aware of the Duke.

She supposed it was because he was so different from any man she had ever met before.

When she had shaken hands with him, she had been aware of a strange vibration.

It was something she did not often feel.

"He has a strong personality," she told herself, "and that is what so many people lack."

But she could not explain to herself exactly what she meant.

When she went back to the Drawing-Room she found herself listening to the intonations of the Duke's voice.

She found it hard not to watch him as he talked to her Father.

She did not stay long, but went upstairs to find Nanny and tell her that they had two extra visitors.

Nanny had been out the whole day visiting a woman who was ill.

She had taken some of the special herbal medicine that Ilesa's Mother had made for people in the village.

When Ilesa went up to her room she found Nanny taking off her bonnet.

"What's all this I hears, Miss Ilesa?" she asked. "Her Ladyship's arrived unexpectedly, and now the Duke of Mountheron! I can hardly believe it!"

"It is true, Nanny," Ilesa said. "Doreen came home just before luncheon, but she is very insistent that we should pretend she arrived two days ago."

Nanny looked surprised.

"Why should she do that, I'd like to know?" she enquired sharply.

"Because, Nanny, she wants to marry the Duke, but she does not want him to think that she is running after him."

"Which I suppose she is!" Nanny finished. "And that doesn't surprise me!"

"Oh, please, Nanny, be very careful because otherwise Doreen will be furious with us, and it is very nice to have her home."

"I suppose she's given you that dress you're wearing," Nanny said. "You certainly looks smart for a change!"

"She *lent* it to me!" Ilesa corrected, "and – what do you think? – Papa and I are driving with the Duke tomorrow to stay at his Country House so that we can see his famous collection of Stubbs' pictures!"

Nanny stared at her for a moment. Then she said:

"Well, that's good news for a change, I must say! It's time you got away from the village and saw a bit of life. From all I've heard, Heron's the right place for seeing a bit of grandeur!"

"That is what I hope to see," Ilesa laughed. "But, Nanny, I have nothing to wear, as you well know."

"We'll just have to find you something, Dearie," Nanny said confidently, "and it's a step in the right direction if Her Ladyship's giving you some of her clothes. She's not given you so much as a cotton handkerchief these last years!"

Nanny spoke tartly.

Ilesa knew she had never really forgiven Doreen for not attending her Stepmother's Funeral.

It had in fact caused a great deal of comment in the village.

Nanny had expressed her views forcibly on a number of occasions.

Doreen, being beautiful and rich, was written up in every newspaper.

Yet she had never made any attempt to help her Father in all he was trying to do.

It was something Ilesa had no wish to comment on at the moment.

Quickly she left Nanny's bedroom and went to her own.

She knew the first problem before they went to Heron was to find something to wear for dinner this evening.

She knew Doreen would be very critical and she could hardly appear downstairs in the same gown she was wearing now.

She looked in her wardrobe and gave a sigh.

She had been busy helping her Father these last two years when he had been so unhappy.

She had not really had time to think about herself or her appearance.

She heard Nanny going into one of the guest-rooms to make up a bed for Doreen.

She would then do the same for the Duke and Ilesa went to help her.

Fortunately, because Nanny was so meticulous, the rooms were clean and dusted.

Ilesa took two vases from her own room. She put one in the room which Doreen was to occupy and the other in the Duke's.

"I expect his groom will valet him, Nanny," she said. "Poor old Briggs will never manage to do that as well as laying the table and giving the silver an extra polish."

"I'll see to that," Nanny said. "Just you go and make yourself look pretty, and I'll do your hair before you goes downstairs."

"Thank you, Nanny," Ilesa answered. "Doreen has already been very critical of my appearance, and I cannot imagine what I am going to wear this evening."

"There's a gown in your Mother's wardrobe as will fit you perfectly!" Nanny said.

Ilesa was still.

"You do not think Papa would mind my wearing Mama's clothes?"

"I doubt he'll even notice," Nanny assured her. "Men are not very perceptive when it comes to women's clothes, and the gown I'm thinking of is a very simple one."

The Vicar had refused to have anything of his wife's removed from the room they had both used.

Ilesa knew that her mother's gowns were all still

hanging in the wardrobe, just as they had always done.

She felt she was somehow intruding on something very sacred.

Then she knew that her Mother, of all people, would want her to look her best if it helped Doreen.

It would certainly seem rather strange if, while she was so smart, her sister looked like a rag-bag.

Anyway there was no time to argue.

By the time Nanny had finished the rooms, Ilesa could hear her Father bringing the Duke upstairs to change for dinner.

She hurried into her own room.

A few seconds later Nanny joined her.

She was carrying a very pretty gown that her Mother had often worn when she and her husband went out to dinner.

It was a very pale mauve, and on Ilesa it made her look like a Parma violet.

Nanny arranged her hair skilfully in the same way that Doreen wore hers.

When Ilesa looked at herself in the mirror, she smiled.

"I see a strange young woman, Nanny," she said, "whom I have never met before!"

"You'll do your Father proud," Nanny said. "I'm not saying more than that."

Ilesa kissed the old woman on the cheek and walked towards the door.

"You had better go and see if you can help Doreen, Nanny," she said. "I am sure she is used to a lady's-maid and half-a-dozen other people to help her."

"It's a pity she doesn't help other people herself!" Nanny answered.

Ilesa smiled.

There was no use arguing with Nanny who always had the last word and she was quite certain she would say the same thing to Doreen.

She hurried down the stairs and was tidying up the Drawing-Room when the Duke came in.

If he looked very impressive in his day-clothes, he was overpowering in evening-dress.

For a moment Ilesa just stood staring at him.

Then she was aware that he was looking at her in the same way.

Quickly, because she felt it was embarrassing to remain silent, she said:

"I hope Your Grace has found everything you want? We do not often have people to stay and Papa would be very upset if you were uncomfortable."

"I have everything I could possibly want," the Duke said, "and you cannot imagine how exciting it was for me to see two pictures by Stubbs which I had always heard of, but had never seen before."

"They are Papa's joy and delight!" Ilesa said. "My grandfather had some very fine pictures by other artists, but of course they now belong to my Uncle Robert."

"I have met your Uncle several times," the Duke said. "I am sure he will be a great success in India, but I understand that closing the house has presented many problems in the village."

Ilesa sighed.

"It has been terrible for Papa," she said. "Most of
the people in the village worked at The Hall and
they had no idea how to find employment elsewhere.
Papa has done his best to help them, but it has not
been easy."

"I heard that from my hosts last night."

"The Marquess has been very kind in taking on
one of the game-keepers. He is such a nice man,
with a wife and five children. He could not possibly
support them on the small pension which was all
Papa could give him."

"Surely your Uncle should have done that?" the
Duke asked.

"He did pension off a lot of the old people, but it
was impossible for him to do the same for everybody. I understand it is very expensive being the
Governor of an Indian Province."

"That is true," the Duke agreed, "but it was
hardly right to leave all the difficulties that have
ensued to your Father!"

He paused before he added:

"And to you! I hear you are doing a lot, too."

"It is only what Mama would have done if she
were still alive," Ilesa said. "And thank you, thank
you very much, for asking Papa to stay at your
house. It will be so good for him to get away and
forget all the troubles his parishioners bring him
every day, however small."

She spoke in a way that showed how much it
meant to her too.

The Duke was thinking how extraordinary it was

that anyone so young and so beautiful should be concerned about the village people.

At the same time as he had realised, being supremely unselfconscious about herself.

He was used to women who flirted with him with every word they spoke, with every movement of their lips and every glance.

Ilesa spoke unaffectedly.

The Duke knew that she was thinking of her Father and not of herself when she talked of going to stay at Heron.

The Vicar joined them and Ilesa said:

"I forgot to tell you, Papa, Mr. Craig's arm is much better. He told me to tell you it was due to Mama's herbs, which he said were 'like a gift from Heaven itself'."

The Vicar smiled.

"That is exceedingly good news! I was afraid he might have to lose his hand."

"I saw it this morning, before I arranged the flowers in the Church," Ilesa said, "and it is healing perfectly."

"Who is Mr. Craig?" the Duke asked.

"He is the Butcher," Ilesa replied. "He was cutting up some meat when his knife slipped, and he sustained the most frightful wound just above his wrist. He lost so much blood that we were afraid he would have to lose his hand."

"And the herbs with which you treated him saved it?" the Duke enquired, as if he was trying to understand.

"They are a special concoction which Mama

always used for emergencies like this. It is very difficult to get a Doctor to come here. Sometimes they refuse to come because there is no chance of their being paid."

"So you have taken their place!" the Duke said.

"I am not nearly as good as Mama was," Ilesa said, "but I am very excited that I have done the right thing where Mr. Craig is concerned."

The Duke was about to ask more when the door opened and Doreen came in.

She was certainly looking fantastic in a gown which must have cost more than the Vicar's annual stipend.

As she glided towards the Duke she glittered in the light of the setting sun.

Ilesa knew she would look marvellous in the light of the candles on the Dining-Room table.

The Duke was watching her curiously and, she thought appreciatively.

'I am sure he will ask her to marry him,' Ilesa thought. 'Then Doreen will really be happy!'

As the thought came to her, she remembered the other man; the man who had loved her for some time.

The man about whom Sir Mortimer Jackson intended to make trouble for her.

"Can Doreen really love two men at the same time?" Ilesa wondered.

Then as she saw her sister look at the Duke in a very flirtatious manner, she reminded herself that she was very young and inexperienced.

There was no point in trying to understand what was going on.

It was not her world.

The world in which she lived and the kind of difficulties that faced her were very different.

They concerned ordinary people whose problem was, quite simply, how to keep alive.

"That is what really matters," she told herself, "and if Doreen becomes a Duchess, it is very unlikely we shall ever see her again."

She saw her sister touch the Duke's arm in an intimate manner which was almost a caress.

"She has won!" Ilesa told herself.

Then she could not help wondering if the Duke had any idea there were other men in her sister's life.

And if he did know – did he mind?

CHAPTER FOUR

The next morning Ilesa awoke early and realised she had not gone to sleep until very late.

She knew it was wrong of her and the memory embarrassed her but she had lain awake wondering if the Duke would go into Doreen's room.

She had heard her sister telling him who slept in which rooms when they went up to bed.

"Papa has the big room at the end," Doreen had said, "which always seems to be out of proportion to the rest of the house. But he and Mama had a kind of Suite with a dressing-room for him and a *Boudoir* for Mama where she wrote her letters."

She smiled sweetly up at the Duke.

"I used to think it very big as a child, but that was before I had been in an enormous house like yours."

She made the words sound caressing, and went on:

"Now, when I come home, I do not sleep in the room where I used to as a child, but in a Guest-Room! As you and I are both guests, our rooms are side by side."

Ilesa had hardly listened to the conversation.

But when she was in bed it came back into her mind.

She had wondered why Doreen was giving the Duke what amounted to a plan of the house.

Now the answer struck her and she was shocked.

It seemed to her horrifying that the Duke should come into her Father's house and behave improperly with her sister.

"I must not think about it! I will not think about it!" she told herself.

But of course she could not banish it from her mind, and it was a long time before she fell asleep.

When the morning came, she was excited by the idea of going to stay at Heron.

Yet in a way she wished the invitation had not been given.

"I shall be out of place there," she told herself. "I have nothing in common with the Duke and his smart friends like Doreen."

However it was too late now to draw back.

Moreover she knew her Father would insist on her being one of the party.

He had arranged the night before that they should leave immediately after Morning Service.

It suited the villagers for it to be early so that they could get home to cook the Sunday luncheon.

That is to say if they could afford one.

It was a fairly long drive to the Duke's house, and he wanted to arrive not too late in the afternoon.

"It is very fortunate," he said, "that I came from London in this large travelling-carriage."

When they climbed into the vehicle, which was

open, the Duke sat on the driving-seat with Doreen beside him.

Ilesa and her Father sat behind.

Behind them was a groom perched rather perilously on a small seat on top of the luggage.

Some of the small cases, including Doreen's hat-box were with Ilesa and her Father.

Because Ilesa had no idea what to take with her, she had left it to Nanny.

Her ancient trunk looked slightly out of place beside Doreen's very elegant luggage.

It was a lovely day and the Duke drove with an expertise which Ilesa knew her Father appreciated.

He was very careful down the twisting lanes which led out of the village.

When they got to the main road he let the horses have their heads.

They stopped for luncheon at an Inn, where the Duke engaged a private room.

They were served a meal far superior to the food they would have had in the Public Dining-Room.

They set off again.

Now Ilesa was looking forward to seeing Heron for the first time.

She remembered reading about it in the Racing Newspapers.

She had seen it illustrated in a magazine that was sometimes passed on to her when her grandfather was alive.

She was sure she had read that it had been built by Robert Adam, or at least restored by him.

It was said to be one of the largest and most

important of the Palladian mansions in the whole country.

'At least I shall see it once,' she thought.

She was certain from the way Doreen had behaved that she and her Father would not be invited to Heron again, when she became the Duchess of Mountheron.

Doreen had been markedly possessive with the Duke.

She seemed to resent it even when he talked of Stubbs' pictures with the Vicar.

She looked furious if he spoke to Ilesa.

Finally they drove in through some impressive wrought-iron gold-tipped gates and up a long avenue of magnificent lime-trees.

Now Ilesa could understand why Doreen was so determined to marry the Duke.

Never had she imagined a house could be so impressive, so enormous.

While at the same time it was such a fitting background for the Duke himself.

The sun was shining on the panes of a multitude of windows.

She thought they flashed a welcome to their owner as he arrived.

Even as they approached, his standard was run up on the flagpole on the roof.

At the same time a carpet was run down a long flight of steps which led up to the front door.

The Duke brought his horses to a standstill and grooms came running to hold their heads.

Then he helped Doreen down from the driving-seat.

She swept up the steps without waiting for her Father or Ilesa, as if the place belonged to her.

The entrance hall was to Ilesa exactly as a hall should be.

It was perfectly proportioned and in the alcoves there were statues of Greek goddesses.

Above the huge, exquisitely carved mantelpiece there hung a number of ancient regimental flags.

They were relics Ilesa guessed, of battles won by the Duke's ancestors.

He had told them at luncheon that his aunt, Lady Mavis, would be acting as his hostess.

"She is my youngest aunt," he said, "and is unmarried, so I find it very convenient that she can stay with me whenever I need a chaperon!"

There was a twist to his lips as he said the last word.

Ilesa thought that if he was having somebody to stay with whom he was having an *affaire de coeur* he would not want his aunt there.

She tried not to think such things.

They only upset her and were foreign to her nature.

Lady Mavis was waiting for them in the very attractive Salon into which they were taken as soon as they entered the house.

She was a very pretty woman of about thirty-five and it seemed sad that she was unmarried.

The Duke however had explained, when he told

them that she would be at Heron, that years ago she had had an unfortunate love-affair.

Her *fiancé* had died tragically, and she had never cared for anybody else.

Lady Mavis was dressed very simply and much more appropriately than Doreen.

Doreen was wearing an elaborate gown in a bright colour which Ilesa thought was entirely out of place in the country.

She was, of course, too tactful to say so.

And when she saw Lady Mavis she knew she had been right.

"I have brought with me some guests, Aunt Mavis," the Duke said, kissing her lightly on the cheek. "I want to introduce you to Doreen's sister Ilesa, and her Father, the Reverend Mark Harle. He is a son of the late Earl of Harlestone and owns two magnificent Stubbs pictures which rival mine!"

"I find that hard to believe!" Lady Mavis replied as she kissed the Duke.

She shook hands with Doreen, saying politely: "How nice to see you again!" before she turned to Ilesa.

She took her hand, then exclaimed:

"I did not know that Lady Barker had a sister, and how lovely you are!"

Ilesa blushed because the compliment was something she had not expected.

Then Lady Mavis shook hands with the Vicar and said:

"It was good of you to come at such short notice.

I am sure my nephew wants to make you envious when you see his collection!"

"I am afraid I shall be very envious," the Vicar said, "however hard I try to resist breaking that particular commandment."

They laughed at that.

Lady Mavis poured out the tea which was waiting for them by the fireplace.

She sat on the sofa in front of the table.

On it were arrayed a silver tea-pot, kettle, milk and cream jugs.

They were all standing on a very fine tray which Ilesa thought must have been made in the reign of George III.

She had learned a lot about silver from her Mother.

She had taught her to recognise the different periods from the silver her grandfather had at The Hall.

The Vicar sat beside Lady Mavis.

Doreen deliberately began what appeared to be a very intimate conversation with the Duke.

This left Ilesa to her own devices.

She looked around the room, appreciating the pictures which were all by famous Artists.

There were also some very fine carved gilt tables which she thought were of the period of Charles II.

She almost started when the Duke said unexpectedly:

"I hope you are admiring this room, Miss Harle. It was my Mother's favourite, and she took all the pieces she liked best from other parts of the house and put them in here."

"I was thinking how beautiful it is," Ilesa replied, "and I especially admire the Charles II tables."

The Duke raised his eye-brows.

"You realised they were Charles II?"

"I thought they must be from the style of the carving, and of course the crown appears on two of them as was usual in his reign."

She thought it was almost an insult that the Duke was surprised that she should be so knowledgeable.

She could not therefore resist saying:

"I think the Van Dyck over the fireplace is one of the finest paintings I have ever seen!"

"Now you are making me determined to show you my Picture Gallery," the Duke said. "When your Father has finished his tea, I suggest we go first to look at my Stubbs collection before we start talking about them."

"You will not have to ask Papa twice to do that!" Ilesa smiled.

The Duke suggested it to the Vicar who got to his feet eagerly.

"I thought you had better see my Stubbs first and get it over," the Duke said. "Otherwise we shall keep talking about something you have not yet seen."

They walked from the Salon.

Only when they were moving down the corridor did Ilesa realise that, as they were leaving, Lady Mavis had asked Doreen to stay with her.

82

She was certain it was something her sister would not wish to do, but she could not refuse.

It was in fact a relief to be able to talk to the Duke without Doreen scowling at her behind his back.

The Duke took them into a room where his Stubbs collection was hung.

There were certainly a great number of them, and he stopped in front of one which was named *Foxhounds in a Landscape, 1762*.

"It is believed Stubbs painted this at Berkeley Castle," he said.

"I have heard that," the Vicar replied.

Then they came to one entitled *Provenance*, which had been commissioned, the Duke said, by the Marquess of Rockingham.

The Vicar was thrilled by the way it was painted with a background of trees and a river.

"The little hut on the far bank," he said, "is repeated in *Mares by an Oak-Tree*."

The Duke gave an exclamation as he said:

"I wondered if you would notice that! I will show you that picture when we reach the other side of the room."

Then as they moved on, it was Ilesa who was the more excited.

The picture they were now looking at was one she had seen reproduced in a magazine.

She had never thought she would be lucky enough ever to see the original.

It was of a cheetah and its two Indian handlers accompanying it.

"Look, Papa! Look!" she said excitedly. "The picture we talked about and you said you would love to own!"

"I had no idea it belonged to Your Grace," the Vicar remarked.

"It is a new acquisition," the Duke explained. "I have only owned it for the last six months."

"But . . it is so . . beautiful!" Ilesa breathed, "and I have always . . longed to see a cheetah!"

She saw the Duke's lips move as if he was about to say something to her.

Then he seemed to change his mind and said:

"It is, in my opinion, one of Stubbs' best paintings. His model was the cheetah presented to George III by Sir George Piggott, who, if you remember, was Governor-General of Madras."

He was speaking to the Vicar who said:

"I have always heard that that cheetah was the very first ever seen in England."

"I am sure that is true," the Duke agreed. "George III gave him into the care of his brother, the Duke of Cumberland, at Windsor Forest, who kept a Menagerie."

The Vicar gave a short laugh.

"I have read of course, of how the Duke staged an experiment in Windsor Great Park, as he wished to see how cheetahs attacked their prey."

"This cheetah," the Duke said, pointing to the animal with his finger, "attacked a stag who drove him off, and the cheetah then escaped into the woods."

"I read that story," the Vicar said. "It killed a fallow deer before it was recaptured."

"I have heard," Ilesa interposed, "that a cheetah is very fast and looks very beautiful when it moves."

"It is," the Duke answered, "and cheetahs are the fastest animals in the world over a short distance. They have, I believe, been known to reach a speed of sixty miles per hour!"

As if he thought they had said enough about cheetahs, he moved to other pictures in his collection.

But Ilesa kept looking back at what she knew had been called 'The Spotted Sphinx'.

There was something about the animal she found very attractive.

She wondered what it would be like to own one as a pet.

They spent a long time in the Stubbs Room then went upstairs to dress for dinner.

The maids had unpacked Ilesa's trunk.

When they asked her what she intended to wear, she found that Nanny had packed only two evening-gowns.

One was the pale mauve one which had belonged to her Mother and which she had worn last night.

The other she had certainly not expected to see. It was her Mother's wedding-gown.

It was the most beautiful of all her Mother had owned, but it would never have occurred to Ilesa to wear it.

It had been made when crinolines were in fashion, but did not have the whalebone underneath it.

It just had a very full skirt sweeping down from a tiny waist.

The whole gown was made of shadow lace, or what Ilesa was told when she was a child was 'fairy lace'.

It was so fine and so delicate that it seemed no more substantial than a spider's web.

She was sure she would look over-dressed in it.

Yet when she put it on, she knew nothing could be more in keeping with the house.

It fitted her perfectly because her figure was similar to her Mother's, and the soft folds of the bertha which revealed her shoulders was very attractive.

She looked very young, very lovely, and as if she had just stepped out of one of the pictures which hung on the walls.

She felt however, a little shy as she went downstairs.

It was a relief to find that there were other guests for dinner.

Two middle-aged couples who were the Duke's neighbours were there.

Also a tall, handsome young man who was introduced to her as Lord Randall.

She knew that this was the man with whom Doreen had been involved at *The Three Feathers*.

He seemed very pleasant.

As Ilesa shook hands with him she knew at once that he was not the wicked villain she had made him out to be in her mind.

She saw him looking at Doreen who followed her a few seconds later into the Salon.

She was immediately convinced that Lord Randall really loved her sister.

Yet because she had no intention of marrying him there was an unmistakable agony in his expression.

From the way Doreen spoke to Lord Randall, Ilesa knew that she had expected him to be there.

She guessed that Doreen had engineered it to prevent Sir Mortimer from making mischief.

She could not help thinking it was cruel of her especially when Doreen went straight to the Duke's side as soon as he came into the room.

It seemed she was doing it to make it clear to everyone that there was an intimacy between them.

When Ilesa found herself sitting next to Lord Randall at dinner she talked to him about the country-side.

She learned that he had a house in Hampshire of which he was very proud.

"It has been in my family for four generations," he said, "but of course it does not compare in any way with Heron."

There was a note of despair in his voice.

As he spoke he looked across the table at Doreen whose beautiful face was turned up to the Duke's.

Ilesa felt very sorry for him.

"How long have you known my sister?" she asked.

"Ever since she first came to London and swept through it like a meteor from the sky!" Lord Randall replied.

Ilesa did not speak and he went on:

"Her beauty stunned me the first moment I saw her. But I suppose I should have known that she is as far out of my reach as the moon."

"She is certainly very beautiful," Ilesa agreed.

"Too beautiful for any man's peace of mind," Lord Randall said.

Now there was a harsh note in his voice.

Because she felt so sorry for him, Ilesa changed the subject and talked about horses.

She was sure that he would be interested in them and hoped that for the moment, at any rate, he would forget Doreen.

Lord Randall told her that the Duke had been his best friend when they were at Eton.

They had bought and broken in many young horses together, and found it an absorbing hobby.

"I suppose Drogo is one of the best riders in England," he said. "Of course he owns the finest horses, but he can make even an inferior animal seem exceptional."

"My Father also has a great love of horses," Ilesa said, "but we cannot afford many and have to be very careful of those we do have."

"Are you saying you are poor?" Lord Randall asked.

"Very poor," Ilesa answered, "but we were fortunate in that when my grandfather was alive, both Papa and I could ride any of the horses in his stable."

"I always had the idea," Lord Randall said, "that Doreen came from a wealthy family which owned a large estate!"

"That was true of my grandfather," Ilesa said,

"but my Father, being the third son, is only the Vicar of Littlestone. I am sure you know as well as I do that Vicars are seldom rich. They have to put their hands in their pockets for a great number of poor people."

"That is true," Lord Randall agreed.

Ilesa was thinking how typical it was of Doreen to have talked of her grandfather's house rather than her Father's.

Of course, as she had married a very rich man, it would be natural for people to assume she had always been brought up in luxury.

When dinner was over, they moved into one of the other Reception Rooms.

It was just as beautiful as the Salon.

The middle-aged guests soon said they must be on their way home.

Therefore everyone was able to go to bed soon after eleven o'clock.

As they went up the stairs, Ilesa thought that Lord Randall was looking longingly at Doreen.

She knew her sister was deliberately avoiding him.

It was in case the Duke should think there was anything unusually familiar about the way they spoke to each other.

When Ilesa went into her bedroom Doreen followed her.

She shut the door. Then she said sharply:

"Where did you get that gown? And why have I not seen it before?"

"Nanny packed it for me," Ilesa said, "and surely you recognise it as Mama's wedding-gown?"

"It is far too elaborate and over-dressed!" Doreen remarked angrily.

As she herself was wearing a gown that had a large bustle and which was decorated with flowers on either side, Ilesa could only stare at her.

"I know what you are thinking," Doreen said, "but I am a married woman and can wear chiffon glittering with diamanté. But girls should not push themselves forward, and certainly not be dressed like someone on the stage!"

"It was either this or one of the gowns I wear at home which are almost in rags!" Ilesa protested. "I had no idea I was going anywhere like this. I was going to ask Papa for a new gown, but he wanted the money for somebody who is sick."

"Well, do not wear that dress again!" Doreen said. "And I saw you talking to Hugo Randall at dinner. What were you saying?"

"We were talking about you," Ilesa said.

"I thought you might be! For Heaven's sake, be careful! If the Duke thought that Hugo and I were close friends, he might be suspicious."

Ilesa was silent for a moment.

Then she said:

"I think Lord Randall loves you very much, Doreen."

"I know that," Doreen said, "and I am fond of him too. But you do see, I must be a Duchess! I must own this enormous house, and the one in Park Lane."

"Can owning houses really make anyone happy?"

Ilesa asked. "I should have thought it was the man who lived in them who was the most important."

There was a little pause before Doreen said:

"I *am* going to marry the Duke! It is just a question of time before he actually asks me, and you be careful what you say to Hugo Randall!"

She went from the room as she spoke.

Ilesa heard her hurrying down the corridor towards her bedroom.

She gave a deep sigh.

She had the feeling that Doreen was not going to be happy and, although she would never admit it, she was making a mistake.

Then she asked herself who was she to judge.

'Nobody has ever proposed to me,' she thought. 'And no one is likely to, as I never meet any men in Littlestone.'

She undressed and got into bed.

Before she fell asleep she tried not to think of her sister and her problems.

Instead she was seeing Stubbs' painting of a cheetah – the Spotted Sphinx – with the Indian handlers beside him.

Ilesa awoke very early as she always did at home.

The sun, peeping between the curtains on the windows, was the pale gold of dawn.

Quite suddenly she thought this was her opportunity to see the gardens and the lake.

She might not be able to do so before she had to go home.

Her Father and the Duke had talked of going to

the stables soon after breakfast, and she would certainly want to go with them.

She dressed herself quickly, finding that Nanny had packed the best of her simple gowns.

They did not compare with anything that Doreen would be wearing.

Ilesa however was not interested in herself, but what she could see.

She slipped down the stairs to find the front door was already open.

There were the sounds of servants brushing the carpets in the nearest rooms.

She walked out into the sunshine, thinking how exciting it was to explore everything on her own.

The gardens were wonderful.

She walked over the lawns past flower-beds and shrubs brilliant with blossom.

There was a Herb-Garden which entranced her.

She thought how much her Mother would have enjoyed seeing it.

Then she came to an iron gate which led out of the garden to an Orchard.

Because it seemed so inviting, she opened the gate and walked through the Orchard.

Then in front of her she saw a wire fence.

As she reached it she wondered if it would prevent her from going any further.

Then she gave a gasp.

On the other side of the fence, lying on the ground, was a large animal.

Ilesa could hardly believe her eyes, but it was a tiger!

CHAPTER FIVE

The Duke had risen early, as he usually did.

Instead of going to the stables, however, as he most often did, he went to his Menagerie.

It was something which always thrilled him and was very close to his heart.

He had learned however, that it was a great mistake to tell people about it.

They either told him that they were terrified of wild animals, or else that it was cruel to keep them cooped up in cages.

He was sick of hearing the same arguments over and over again.

The fact that Menageries had been in existence since the time of Julius Caesar did not impress them.

He therefore had put his Menagerie well out of sight of any guests who wandered in the gardens.

He kept it entirely for his own enjoyment.

He planned to expand it year by year.

That would mean his going abroad to buy the animals he particularly wanted to include in his collection.

It was half-past-six as he walked out through the

front door, passing two maids in mob-caps who were scrubbing the steps.

He walked through the gardens, appreciating their beauty.

Then he went through a door in the Herb-Garden and down into the Orchard.

The fruit-trees were breathtakingly beautiful with pink and white blossom.

As he looked at them they reminded him of how Ilesa had looked last night.

He had been stunned by her beauty when he first saw her in the Vicarage.

But wearing a picture-gown which he recognised as being out of date, she looked as if she belonged to a different era.

He was still thinking of her as he reached the enclosure of his favourite animal – a tiger called Rajah.

He had brought him back from India as a cub and trained him himself.

Rajah was inclined to be fierce, and he made the men who looked after him nervous.

They never entered his enclosure alone.

When he was fed there was always another man standing by with a sharp-pronged weapon with which if necessary to hold him at bay.

The Duke walked to the entrance and lifted the bolt.

It was locked at night, but it was always opened at dawn so that he could go in and see the animals as early as he wished.

Then as he shut the door of the enclosure behind him, he looked for Rajah.

Instantly he was stunned into immobility.

He could see Rajah lying under one of the trees, but he thought he must be dreaming.

The tiger's head was in the lap of a woman sitting beside him. She was stroking the tiger's head.

For a moment he thought he must be imagining the picture he saw.

Then he was aware that the woman stroking Rajah was Ilesa!

The Duke did not move. He merely called in a very low voice:

"Rajah! Rajah!"

The tiger raised his head.

Then slowly, almost reluctantly, he rose to his feet and walked towards the Duke.

As he did so the Duke said in a low voice:

"Get out of the enclosure immediately, but do not make any sudden movement!"

Ilesa did not move. She merely smiled at him.

Rajah had reached the Duke and rubbed against him like a cat, making what were purring noises.

Then just as he had done as a cub, he rose on his hind legs and put his front paws on the Duke's shoulders.

The Duke patted him and talked to him.

But he was aware all the time that Ilesa had not obeyed him.

Again he said to her in a different tone of voice from what he had used to the tiger:

"Do as I say!"

She shook her head.

"I am quite safe," she said. "He knows that I love him and he would never hurt me."

The Duke stared at her incredulously.

Then the tiger demanded his attention and he patted and caressed him.

At last the animal went down on the ground and rubbed his body against his legs.

It was then Ilesa got to her feet and said:

"He is the most beautiful creature I have ever seen! I did not know his name, but Rajah is a very fitting one for him."

She was talking as she walked towards the Duke.

When she reached him she bent down to caress the tiger, moving her hand over his head and down his back.

"How can you own anything so beautiful?" she asked. "And even more exciting than your pictures?"

The tiger turned from the Duke to rub his head against Ilesa.

She put her arms round him and kissed the top of his head.

"You are a beautiful, beautiful boy!" she said, "and Rajah is the right name for you."

"I am afraid his keepers have translated it into 'Rajee'," the Duke said. "They are Indian, and it seems to them more appropriate for a tiger."

Ilesa laughed.

As she did so the Duke said:

"Is this really happening? Can you and I be talking across an animal that is supposed to be very fierce?"

"I am sure he is fierce only because people do not understand him," Ilesa said. "Of course he should be treated with respect, and admired."

She turned the tiger's face up to hers.

"Is that not true, Rajah?" she asked. "You want people to admire you and think how important you are."

The Duke still thought he was dreaming.

Then he said:

"I have other animals to show you, if you are interested."

"Of course I am," Ilesa replied. "Why did you not tell me you had a Menagerie?"

"I always keep it a secret," the Duke answered, "but as you have discovered it for yourself, I would like to show you my cheetahs."

Ilesa gave a little cry.

"Cheetahs? You really do have them?"

"I really and truly do," the Duke replied with a smile.

Ilesa patted Rajah again and the Duke did the same.

Then they walked through the gate, leaving the tiger standing watching them go.

"I have had Rajah since he was a cub, and I trained him," the Duke said. "But I have never before known him to allow a stranger to enter his enclosure."

Ilesa did not answer and he asked:

"Have you always had this power over animals?"

"I have never met a tiger before," Ilesa answered, "nor a cheetah, for that matter, but I can manage the most obstreperous horse. I used to help my grandfather's grooms break in those that were really wild."

"I find it hard to believe that what you say is the truth," the Duke said. "How can you look as you do, and yet ride wild horses and make love to savage tigers?"

Ilesa laughed and it was a very pretty sound.

"That is the nicest compliment I have ever had!" she said. "But then, I have not had many!"

The Duke was certain this was true.

He had never met anyone so unselfconscious.

Ilesa talked to him in a manner that was quite different from the way other women did.

They walked round the tiger's enclosure and came to another.

When she saw what it contained Ilesa gave a cry of sheer joy.

Moving among the trees in a large enclosure was a cheetah as beautiful as the one in the Stubbs picture.

His coat was sleek like that of a short-haired dog, with black spots that were fluffy, like that of a cat's fur.

"This is Che-Che, as the Indian keepers insist on calling him," the Duke said. "His wife Me-Me is hiding from us in the bushes because she has just had four cubs."

"This is the most thrilling thing that has ever happened to me!" Ilesa said.

"The cubs were born only four days ago," the

Duke said, "so I doubt if Me-Me will come to speak to us. But first you must meet Che-Che."

Standing up on the gate, he asked jokingly:

"I suppose you are not too afraid to be introduced to him?"

"That is a gratuitous insult!" Ilesa protested.

They walked into the enclosure, and Che-Che ran towards the Duke, welcoming him as a dog or a cat might have done.

He was purring loudly as he moved his body against the Duke's legs. Then he jumped up and began to lick his face.

Finally, as the Duke caressed him, the cheetah began to nibble at his ear.

"That is the greatest compliment a cheetah can pay you," he said in a quiet voice.

Ilesa put out her hand.

To the Duke's surprise the Cheetah turned towards her and started to lick her face.

"You are now accepted as one of the family," the Duke said, "and perhaps Me-Me will let us look at her cubs."

He walked towards a clump of bushes, calling "Me-Me! Me-Me!" as he did so.

There was a pause.

Then a very beautiful cheetah, a little smaller than Che-Che, peeped out.

She did not come any nearer, but the Duke went to her.

As he patted and caressed her, he moved the leaves of the bush to one side so that Ilesa could see the cubs.

They were rather like silver-backed jackals, with a furry spotted under-carriage and a long fluffy mane on their heads.

They were very small and sweet.

Ilesa wanted to pick one up in her arms, but thought it would be a mistake until Me-Me knew her better.

They stayed for some time with the cheetahs.

Then they said good-bye to them both and the Duke took Ilesa to see his monkey-cage.

It was built high enough to enclose several trees, up which the monkeys could climb.

In all the enclosures there were huts where the animals could go if it was cold in the Winter.

The monkey-cage was so large that Ilesa learnt that it covered two acres of ground.

"How can you keep anything so exciting all to yourself?" she asked.

"There are few people – and I thought no women – who enjoy it like you!" the Duke replied. "Let me show you the rest of my family, which I intend to increase year by year."

He had a hippopotamus, lying in a deep pool.

It refused to come out but lay looking like some huge giant in the cool water.

There were two giraffes, one of them quite small, the other very tall.

There was also a black panther which the Duke refused to allow Ilesa to go near.

"He has been with me only for a few months," he said, "and he has already attacked two of the men who look after him. I therefore absolutely forbid you – and I mean this, Ilesa – to go into his enclosure!"

Ilesa did not notice that he had used her Christian name for the first time.

She looked up at him with shining eyes as she asked:

"What will happen if I disobey you?"

"Apart from the fact that the panther might spoil your beauty, I should be very angry and probably would put you in a cage in my Menagerie, so that you can never escape."

Ilesa laughed.

"I would be quite happy if I could play with Rajah and Che-Che every day, and perhaps I will grow fur like theirs to protect me when it is cold!"

The Duke did not answer.

He was thinking that nothing could be more attractive than her hair.

Glittering in the sun it was like a halo round her small pointed face.

As they left the panther the Duke said:

"I am afraid that is where my Menagerie ends at the moment. But I intend to make it very much bigger, and I have been wondering if it would be possible to include bears and even elephants."

Ilesa clapped her hands.

"But of course you must do that! It would not be complete without an elephant. Think how majestic you would look riding it around the grounds!"

The Duke laughed.

"I had not thought of that!"

"It would certainly surprise your neighbours when they came to call."

"Then they will want to see the rest of my Menagerie," the Duke said, "and I want to keep it to myself."

"I need not point out that you are being very selfish," Ilesa answered, "and, please, may I go round again later today in case I never see it again?"

"Would that be such a disaster?" the Duke asked.

"To me it would be a catastrophe!" Ilesa replied. "So, please, be kind and let me enjoy every moment of the Menagerie while I can."

The Duke thought that most women liked to be with him rather than with his possessions, but he replied:

"You shall have your wish, on one condition."

"What is that?" Ilesa enquired.

"That you do not tell your sister or anyone else that you have been here."

"I would certainly not tell Doreen," Ilesa said. "She is terrified of animals, and even dislikes my dogs."

She spoke without thinking, then thought what she had said was unkind.

"She loved your house," she said quickly, "and I can understand that, because it is so magnificent."

"I like to think of it as my *home*," the Duke said, as if he was correcting her.

"But naturally you think like that," Ilesa agreed. "Anywhere where we have been born and where we have been happy with our parents is home, whether it be a cottage or a mansion as spectacular as Heron!"

"Are you saying that you really prefer the Vicarage, which I admit is very attractive, to Heron?"

Ilesa put her head on one side as if she was thinking. Then she said:

"You are trying to institute an impossible comparison. The Vicarage is part of me. It is where I have been blissfully happy ever since I was a child. It is difficult to think of it apart from myself."

She smiled before she continued:

"But Heron is undoubtedly the most magnificent, and at the same time the most beautiful house I have ever seen, so you are very, very lucky!"

The Duke laughed.

"That is a clever and well-thought-out answer!" he said. "And of course I stand corrected for having asked the question."

Ilesa smiled and there were dimples in her cheeks as she said:

"I think actually you were trying to catch me out because you were so surprised that I could make friends with Rajah. Please, can we see him once more before we go back to the house?"

"Of course," the Duke agreed.

They went back to Rajah's enclosure and he bounded towards them as if he was a child running towards his parents.

He was purring even more loudly than he had before.

As the Duke and Ilesa made a fuss of him, he

103

turned from one to the other as if he wanted to express his affection for both of them.

Once, as they were both running their hands through the fur down Rajah's back the Duke unintentionally touched Ilesa's.

Unexpectedly she felt a strange sensation sweep through her.

She looked up at him and their eyes met.

Somehow it was impossible to look away.

Then in a voice that seemed to come from a far distance the Duke said:

"You are a very unusual person, Ilesa! I have never met anyone at all like you before."

"I think perhaps that is because you never meet anyone ordinary," Ilesa replied. "I live in the country, but I love animals. And I am very very fortunate, because they love me!"

"That is not surprising," the Duke said.

Then as if Rajah was annoyed that he was losing their attention, he nibbled the Duke's ear.

They had been a long time with the animals.

When they got back to the house the Butler informed the Duke that the Vicar and Lady Mavis had waited for a while after breakfast, but had then gone riding.

"That was sensible," the Duke said. "Miss Harle and I will have breakfast at once, and tell the grooms to bring the horses round in half-an-hour."

"Am I really going to be able to ride one of your magnificent horses?" Ilesa asked.

"You made it very obvious to me at the Vicarage that that was what you wanted," the Duke replied.

"I will go and change," she said, "just in case I keep you waiting. I know that is an unpardonable sin!"

She did not wait for the Duke's reply, but heard him laugh as she ran up the stairs.

Her riding-habit was old and certainly not what might have been expected at Heron.

But because she was in such a hurry to ride Ilesa did not think about her appearance.

She pinned up her hair in a tidy manner as she always did when she went out hunting.

She put on the hat which also was old, but had a pretty blue gauze veil round the crown.

It was, although she did not realise it, something that was rapidly going out of fashion.

But it had been correct fifteen years ago when her mother had first bought it.

It was certainly very becoming, the Duke thought as she hurried into the Breakfast-Room with shining eyes.

He knew how excited she was at being able to ride one of his horses.

Because she was anxious to ride, Ilesa ate her breakfast very quickly.

As the Duke put down his cup of coffee she finished hers.

"Come along," he said, "the horses will be waiting for us, and I am waiting to see if you are as proficient a rider as you would have me believe."

"It will be very humiliating if I am thrown at the first fence!" Ilesa said. "But I did not mean to boast."

"After what I saw this morning," the Duke said, "you are entitled to boast as much as you wish and I would not allow anyone to contradict you."

"I may have to keep you to that promise," Ilesa replied.

She ran down the steps outside the front door and saw the grooms holding two superb horses.

They were certainly finer than anything she had ridden from her grandfather's stable.

She knew that, if her Father was riding an equally fine animal, he would be in his element.

The Duke lifted her into the saddle and skilfully arranged her riding-skirt over the pommel.

Then almost before he could mount, Ilesa was riding away.

She knew she was on the finest horse she had ever ridden or even imagined.

There was no need to express her excitement and delight.

The Duke could see it on her face.

They had ridden onto some level ground on the other side of the Park, when without really arranging to do so, they were racing each other.

The horses knew what was expected of them.

When they reached the end of a very long field they were running neck and neck.

It would have been impossible to say who was ahead.

As they drew in their horses, Ilesa said:

"That was the most exciting thing I have ever done. Oh, thank you! Thank you! It is something I will always remember."

"I hope," the Duke said quietly, "that it is something we will do very often."

She thought he was reassuring her that she would be invited again to Heron when he married Doreen.

She told herself however, it was something she could not count on.

She was quite certain that once Doreen had become a Duchess she would, as she had done before, forget about her family.

She would certainly not invite them to Heron.

They rode on, and their horses flew over the jumps as if they were birds.

When finally they turned for home, Ilesa said:

"Thank you, thank you again! There are no words in which to tell you what a wonderful morning it has been and how happy you have made me!"

"I may have played a small part in it, but your thanks should really go to Rajah and Che-Che, and of course to Skylark, on whom you are sitting at the moment."

Ilesa bent forward to pat her horse's neck.

"He is perfection!" she exclaimed. "I think really he has been ridden across the sky, by one of the gods, perhaps carrying a message to Olympus."

"You do not think of yourself as a goddess?" the Duke asked dryly.

Ilesa smiled.

"You have forgotten that I am just a country bumpkin who lives amongst the cabbages and turnips. It is only your magic wand that has transplanted me for the moment into a Paradise I did not even know existed."

"Then that is where you will have to stay," the Duke said.

As they reached the level ground they were racing each other again.

Doreen was just coming down the stairs as they arrived.

When she saw that the Duke was alone with her sister there was a darkness in her eyes.

It told Ilesa immediately that she was furious.

"Where have you been?" she asked sharply. "I was told that Papa and Lady Mavis waited for you, then rode off without you."

"I was in the garden," Ilesa said lamely.

"It was my fault," the Duke said. "I insisted on your sister coming back to her rather late breakfast with me. Then we went riding, but somehow missed finding your Father and my aunt."

Doreen did not reply, but as they went towards the Salon she slipped her arm through the Duke's.

"There are so many things I want you to show me," she said in her most caressing voice. "And I shall feel very neglected if you refuse."

"You know I will not do that," the Duke said, "and of course there must be things which will interest your Father."

As he spoke Lord Randall came down the passage.

"You will hardly believe it, Drogo," he said, "but I overslept and I suppose I have missed all the fun."

"All of it!" the Duke replied. "That will teach you not to drink so much at night."

Lord Randall laughed.

"I admit I am not as abstemious as you. At the same time, I am regretting that I did not ride with you this morning."

"Let us make plans for what we are going to do this afternoon," the Duke said.

They had reached the Salon by this time and the Vicar said:

"Good morning, Your Grace! I hope you did not mind our going ahead of you, but we expected you to catch up with us."

"I must have gone in a different direction," the Duke replied vaguely, "but now I would like you to tell me what you want to do this afternoon."

He paused a moment and then went on:

"Personally I would like to show you my race-horses. The Yearlings are trained here before they go to Newmarket, and I think you will enjoy seeing them."

"I shall indeed," the Vicar agreed, "and Ilesa must come with us because she is very knowledgeable on breeding."

The Duke looked at her in surprise.

"*Another* talent?" he asked.

"Papa is flattering me," Ilesa answered. "I read aloud the *Racing Times*, so I know quite a lot about your race-horses and how they have carried off all the important prizes giving no one else a chance."

The Duke laughed.

Ilesa was aware once again that her sister was looking at her with fury.

"I am sure," Doreen said now in the sweetest of tones, "that Papa will not want to be away from his beloved Parishioners for long. So, if he and Ilesa are leaving tomorrow, *we* must, Drogo dear, show them everything of importance today."

She emphasised the word '*We*'.

It was then Lady Mavis said:

"I, too, would like to come with you to see your horses, Drogo, and I am quite certain that Lord Randall will want to come too."

"I refuse to be left out!" Hugo Randall said. "Why do we not get your Phaetons out of the store, Drogo? I will race you as we have done before, and this time, I intend to have the best team!"

The Duke laughed.

"That is a challenge! All right, that is what we will do."

They walked round the garden, then had an early luncheon.

Ilesa hurried upstairs to put on her hat.

She gave only a passing thought to the fact that Doreen was looking as if she was going to a Royal Garden-Party.

What did looks matter when she could ride the Duke's horses and see his Yearlings?

She came downstairs again and walked into the Salon.

Only the Duke and Doreen were there.

As she entered the room Ilesa was aware that Doreen had her arms around the Duke's neck and was pulling his head down for him to kiss her.

Ilesa stood still, feeling embarrassed at having interrupted them.

Then she knew that they were not aware of her presence.

"Not here, Doreen!" she heard the Duke say sharply.

CHAPTER SIX

They spent the afternoon very enjoyably as planned, seeing the Yearlings being trained, and watching the Duke and Lord Randall winning one race each in the Phaetons.

When they were going upstairs to dress for dinner Ilesa said to her Father in a low voice:

"Are we leaving tomorrow?"

The Vicar shook his head.

"No," he said. "I had intended to do so, but plans have changed."

Ilesa looked surprised and he said:

"The Duke has asked me to help him with the alterations to his Private Chapel."

Ilesa was listening, and he went on:

"It was actually first built in Tudor times, then it was destroyed by the Puritans and reconstructed during the reign of Charles II."

"It sounds fascinating!" Ilesa said.

"It is," the Vicar agreed, "and Adam was wise enough to leave it alone. Unfortunately early in this century some time before Queen Victoria came to the throne, the reigning Duke enlarged the Chapel."

He gave a short laugh as he said:

"As you can imagine, the additions he made were completely alien to the Chapel of the Restoration Period."

"So you are going to advise him on restoring it," Ilesa said.

"The builders are coming tomorrow afternoon to see the Duke to discuss plans for the alterations," the Vicar said. "Then we can go home the following day."

Ilesa wanted to say that delighted her because then she would be able to be with Rajah and Che-Che again.

"You must come to look at the Chapel," her Father was saying. "It is one of the few private Chapels in England still existing where anyone can be married without having to have a Special Licence from the Archbishop of Canterbury."

"Like the Mayfair Chapel!" Ilesa exclaimed.

"That is right," the Vicar agreed.

Ilesa went to her bedroom thrilled that they were to stay another whole day at Heron.

She had however a problem concerning what she was to wear that evening.

The Duke had told them before they went upstairs that he had lent the Ball-Room to one of his Cousins who was giving a party for young people.

"They are seventeen and eighteen years old," the Duke explained, "but we old 'fuddy-duddies' can go in later and dance to the Orchestra."

He was looking at Ilesa as he spoke.

She clasped her hands together as she said:

113

"Oh, that would be wonderful! I have never been to a Ball. I only remember the children's parties that I was too old for after Mama died. But it would be exciting to dance in your Ball-Room!"

"Then I insist on your celebrating your first appearance at a Ball by dancing with me."

She dropped him a mocking curtsy.

"I am honoured, Your Grace!"

Then she was aware that Doreen was looking at her in a hostile fashion.

Hurriedly she joined her Father who she knew was going upstairs.

Now as she entered her bedroom she was wondering if it would look too obvious if she wore her Mother's wedding-gown again.

To her surprise, however, the Housekeeper, a rather formidable person, was in her bedroom.

"I've been hearin' that you're going to the party tonight, Miss," she said, "an' I was just wondering what you'd wear."

"I was wondering the same thing," Ilesa smiled. "But I do not have very much choice."

"I realise that," the Housekeeper answered, "an' I thought, seeing what a picture you made last night in that pretty lace gown, whether you'd like to have another one of th' same period."

Ilesa looked at her in surprise and the Housekeeper explained:

"I've got His Grace's Mother's gown she wore when she was about the same age as yourself and in which she was painted."

As the Housekeeper spoke she took it off the bed.

Ilesa saw that it was a gown of pale pink in exactly the same style that Queen Victoria wore when she came to the throne.

It had a very full skirt and a bertha which revealed the shoulders.

The skirt was ornamented on either side with tiny pink roses.

The satin sash which encircled the waist fastened at the back with a large bow.

"It is lovely!" Ilesa exclaimed. "May I really wear it?"

"I think you'll find it fits," the Housekeeper said. "If not, the Seamstress can quickly alter it so to speak. If she stitches it on you, Emily will be waiting to undo it when you come to bed."

"Oh, thank you, thank you!" Ilesa cried. "It is the prettiest gown I have ever seen!"

After she had her bath the maids helped her into the gown.

Ilesa thought when she looked in the mirror she was like someone out of a picture.

The Housekeeper had asked the Gardeners for some pink roses and arranged them at the back of her head.

When Ilesa went downstairs she felt that she was walking on air and part of a Fairy Story.

At the same time something the Housekeeper had told her was very much in her mind.

She had asked:

"You are quite certain His Grace will not

mind my wearing something that belonged to his Mother?"

"I doubt he'd remember it," the Housekeeper replied. "His Grace lost his Mother when he was only ten years old. Although he was brought up by his Aunts, nothing can take the place of one's own Mother."

"That is very true," Ilesa agreed, "and I miss mine every day."

"His Grace looked unhappy for years," the Housekeeper answered, "and we felt really sorry for the little boy."

This story made Ilesa see the Duke in an entirely new light.

Now, as she neared the Salon door, she was not thinking of him as important, distinguished and rather overwhelming.

Instead, she saw him as a small boy, lost and sad without his Mother.

When she entered the room, everybody was there except for Doreen.

As she walked towards them there was a silence.

Then the Vicar asked:

"Is this really my younger daughter?"

"It is, Papa!" Ilesa smiled. "I have to thank His Grace's kind Housekeeper for finding me this beautiful evening-gown."

"You look lovely," Lady Mavis told her, "absolutely lovely!"

Lord Randall said the same thing.

The Duke said nothing and Ilesa looked at him questioningly.

She saw a strange expression in his eyes she did not understand.

"Y.you do not . . mind my . . borrowing . . it?" she asked anxiously.

"You not only grace my house," the Duke replied, "but will undoubtedly be the Belle of the Ball!"

Ilesa laughed.

"I am afraid you are flattering me. I only hope it comes true."

Doreen arrived a few minutes later, obviously intending to make a dramatic entrance.

Her gown was very different from the one she had worn the night before.

Of a deep emerald green, it accentuated the whiteness of her skin, as did the large emerald necklace she wore.

Both the younger men complimented her on her appearance.

Ilesa knew however, when she looked at her that she was extremely angry.

As on the previous night, there were other guests for dinner.

They were fortunately announced before Doreen could express her opinion of her sister's appearance.

As the newcomers were all hunting people, they talked of their horses and of their plans for the coming Autumn.

The dinner passed with everybody in a very good humour.

When dinner was over and the ladies retired, Ilesa managed to keep away from her sister.

Lady Mavis said to her:

"You look lovely, and I am so delighted that you and your Father can stay another day. I am sure he will be of great help to my nephew in his plans for the Chapel."

"Papa is very knowledgeable on historic buildings," Ilesa agreed.

"He seems to be very knowledgeable about everything!" Lady Mavis smiled. "And he rides so well! I am sure you are very proud of him."

"I only wish that Papa could have a few horses as good as the Duke's," Ilesa said wistfully. "Two of those we have are growing old, and I cannot see how we shall ever be able to replace them."

"I think it is tragic," Lady Mavis said, "that someone who is as outstanding a horseman as your Father should not be able to afford the best horses."

When the gentlemen joined the ladies the Duke said:

"We must all go now to the Ball-Room. My Cousin is expecting us, and I do not think, as her guests are so young, that the Orchestra will play into the early hours of the morning."

"I thought my dancing days were over," the Vicar said, "but actually I am looking forward to waltzing in your Ball-Room, which I am told is as magnificent as the rest of your house!"

"Adam certainly did his best when he designed it," the Duke said. "Having said that, I will leave you to judge for yourself."

To Ilesa, it was the most beautiful room she had ever seen.

The white pillars were touched with gold, the

painted ceiling had huge crystal chandeliers hanging from it.

The polished floor seemed to invite one to dance and it was, she thought, all part of her Fairy Tale.

Doreen was waiting for the Duke to ask her to dance after he had introduced his party to their hostess.

But he said:

"This counts as a 'Coming Out' Ball for your sister, and I claim the right to be her first partner."

Doreen's eyes darkened.

But before she could say anything, Lord Randall put his arm round her waist and swept her onto the floor.

The Orchestra was playing an inviting Waltz, and Ilesa felt as if she was dancing on the clouds.

The Duke was an excellent dancer and as they swung round he said:

"You are so light, I feel as if you have wings on your feet."

"That is just what I was thinking myself," Ilesa answered, "and this is very, very exciting for me!"

Her eyes were shining and her hair glittered golden in the light of the candles.

She thought as the Duke swept her round the room that if she never danced with anyone again, she would never forget this moment.

Nor would she ever forget the beauty of their surroundings and how handsome he was.

After that she danced with Lord Randall.

Eventually the party ended with a Cotillion in which there were presents for all the young girls.

119

They looked like flowers in their pretty Ball-Gowns.

It was not quite midnight when Ilesa went to bed.

She decided she would get up early so that she could spend as much time as possible with Rajah and Che-Che.

.   .   .   .

As she had taught herself to do, Ilesa awoke early.

The sun was just breaking in the East and sweeping away the last of the evening stars.

The sky was clear by the time she reached the garden.

Although she longed to stand and look at the flowers and linger in the Herb-Garden, she felt as if Rajah and Che-Che were calling her.

The joy of being with them was something she knew she would never have again.

She ran through the Orchard.

When she reached Rajah's enclosure, she saw him under the big tree just as he had been the day before.

She opened the gate and started talking to him.

It was in the very special tone she always used to animals.

She sat down on the ground beside him and put her arms round his neck.

"You are so beautiful!" she said. "I shall think about you when I go home and send you messages which I feel somehow you will hear."

The tiger seemed to understand and he nuzzled up against her.

Then as she stroked him she heard the lock click and the Duke came into the pen.

"I thought I would find you here," he said.

He walked towards her and to Ilesa's surprise Rajah did not get up.

He waited until the Duke sat down on the other side of him.

Then he turned his head towards him.

"I came early," Ilesa said, "because I could not bear to lose any time when I could be with Rajah and Che-Che."

She gave a little sigh.

"I shall miss them when I go home."

"As I am sure they will miss you," the Duke said.

"They will have . . you!" Ilesa replied.

"And I shall miss you too," he answered.

There was silence.

Then because Ilesa was aware that something was on his mind, she looked up at him.

"I was just wondering," the Duke said quietly, "what you are going to do about us."

Ilesa was very still.

"I . . I do not . . know what . . you mean," she said after a moment.

"I think you do," the Duke answered. "I fell in love with you, Ilesa, the first moment I saw you. I could not believe anyone could be so beautiful, so unspeakably lovely!"

"I . . it cannot be . . true," Ilesa murmured.

"It is true," he said, "and now I am asking you – no – begging you to marry me."

He was looking at Ilesa as he spoke and her eyes met his.

For a moment her whole face was transformed into a radiance that was like the sun itself.

It was as if she was transported out of time and space into the Fairy Tale world in which she believed.

Then as the Duke watched her spellbound, the radiance faded.

In a voice that seemed to come from a long way away she said:

"D.Doreen! It is . . Doreen you . . are to . . marry!"

The Duke shook his head.

"I had no intention whatever of marrying your sister, or anyone else for that matter. I have never asked a woman to marry me, but I cannot live without you, Ilesa, and that is the truth."

As he spoke he put his arm over Rajah and along Ilesa's shoulders.

Then, she was not quite sure how it happened, but his lips were on hers.

It was the first time she had ever been kissed, and it was everything she had expected, and more.

She felt as if the sunshine was streaking through her breasts.

Her whole body responded to the vibrations she had always felt from the Duke.

In a way she did not understand she was a part of him.

Then he set her free and they just looked into each other's eyes with Rajah purring between them.

"I . . I love you," Ilesa said. "I did not know it was . . love . . but it is . . and it is . . so . . wonderful!"

"That is all I want to know," the Duke replied. "Now, my darling, you can share Rajah with me. I cannot believe many people have kissed for the first time across the back of a tiger!"

Ilesa gave a tremulous little laugh.

Then once again she turned her face away from him.

"But Doreen . . is longing to . . marry you," she said. "She is . . determined to . . marry you. How can I be . . so . . unkind to . . her?"

The Duke put out his hand and took hers.

"I have told you, my Darling," he said, "that I never intended to marry anyone, and certainly not somebody like Doreen."

"But . . but she . . thinks you . . l.love her," Ilesa stammered.

The way she said it told the Duke without words what she was thinking.

"Listen, my Precious," he said, "I can understand because you are so innocent and unspoiled that you are shocked that women like your sister should have *affaires de coeur* with men when they are married, or have been married, to somebody else."

The colour flooded into Ilesa's cheeks and she dropped her head because she could not look at him.

His fingers tightened on hers as he went on:

"You must understand that to most men women are like lovely flowers. We would be inhuman if we

123

did not admire their beauty and enjoy their fragrance and want to possess them, if only for a short while."

"But . . surely . . that is . . wrong?" Ilesa asked.

"Not if the two people concerned both know exactly what they are doing. And if the woman is not a young girl like yourself, but is already married. Although it may seem reprehensible that she is being unfaithful to her husband."

"Papa would . . say that was . . wrong!" Ilesa argued.

"And he would be entirely right in thinking so," the Duke said. "But it is something that has happened since the beginning of time. What I am trying to tell you, my Sweet One, is that every man has in his heart a shrine where he puts first his Mother, then the first woman he really loves. That, if he is fortunate, is his wife! He wants her to be perfect and to belong to him, and only to him."

He paused before he added:

"That is what he is searching for from the time he grows up, even if he does not want to admit it. But of course, as you will understand, he has disappointments. He thinks he has found the perfect flower, the pure lily which should be put in the shrine beside his Mother, only to be disillusioned."

Ilesa was listening and she thought it very touching.

From the way he spoke and the sincerity in his voice, she knew how much his Mother had meant to him.

"I have looked and looked for you," the Duke

went on, "only to find out I was mistaken each time, and the flower that I picked so eagerly had faded."

His voice deepened as he said:

"Now I have found you, and I can hardly believe you are real and not just a part of my imagination, and my dreams."

"I am . . real!" Ilesa said. "But . . why . . oh . . why do you . . have to . . be a . . .Duke? Why could you . . not have been an . . ordinary man whom I . . could love . . look after and make . . happy?"

The Duke thought it was the most touching thing he had ever heard.

He was well aware that the women like Doreen who pursued him and schemed to marry him were attracted by his title far more than they were by him as a man.

Some had wept bitterly when he left them.

At the same time, he could not help being cynically aware of the truth.

Their tears would not have been so bitter if he had not been a Duke as well as an ardent lover.

When he looked across Rajah at Ilesa, he knew she was everything he had searched for; everything he wanted.

Now he realised it was something for which he would have to fight.

For the first time in his life, it was going to be difficult to make a woman do what he wanted.

Where Ilesa was concerned it was against her conscience, or perhaps her soul.

He held her hand in both of his as if he was afraid she might escape him.

Then he said:

"I do not want to upset or worry you, my Darling, but I swear to you that I will never rest until I have made you my wife."

He smiled at her before he went on:

"Somehow we will cope with the problems together, but I will not – I cannot – lose you."

There was a pause and Ilesa said in a very small voice:

"It is . . not only . . Doreen . . but since . . Mama died Papa has been so . . unhappy . . and I know I could . . not . . leave him all . . by himself in . . the Vicarage . . with everybody . . knocking on the . . door with their . . problems . . and . . he would . . have to . . manage . . alone."

She drew in her breath before she said:

"It would be . . cruel and . . wicked for me to . . do so . . and Mama would be very . . unhappy."

"Your Father can have the choice of any parish, any living as my gift, and there are a great number of them."

Ilesa shook her head.

"He will never . . leave Littlestone. The people there . . rely on him to . . help them and . . Papa has known them ever since he was . . born in the Big House . . and grew up . . amongst them."

She turned to look at the Duke and there were tears in her eyes.

"H.how . . how could I . . go away and leave him at . . this moment? Oh . . please . . please . . understand."

The Duke did not speak and she said even more piteously:

"When you . . kissed me . . I knew that I . . loved you . . and I know . . now that what I have been . . feeling ever since . . I came to . . Heron when everything we . . did was so exciting . . and wonderful . . was really . . love."

The Duke did not speak and she went on:

"How . . how could I . . make you happy . . or be as you . . want me to be . . if I knew I had deserted Papa?"

The Duke passed his hand over his forehead.

"Somehow," he said confidently, "we will find a solution. I do not yet know what it is, but I will find one."

He spoke with a determination and in a voice she had never heard before.

Then he said:

"You have to understand, my Lovely, that I will be suffering all the agonies of the damned if I have to think for one moment that I am going to lose you."

Ilesa made a helpless little gesture.

"What . . can I . . do? Oh . . what can I . . do?"

The Duke rose to his feet and walking round Rajah he pulled her to hers.

"We are going to solve this problem together," he said, "but for the moment, no one but Rajah shall know that I love you and that you love me – though not as much as you will love me when I teach you about love. My Darling, my Precious, my little wife-to-be, you are mine, and nobody shall take you from me."

The words ended on a triumphant note.

Then his arms closed round Ilesa and he kissed her fiercely, possessively and passionately, until they were both breathless.

He raised his head and Ilesa hid her face against his shoulder as he said:

"My Darling, I will be very gentle with you. I have no wish to frighten you but, please, be kind to me. I need not only your love, but your kindness and understanding of how much I am suffering, and how afraid I am that you will go away from me."

"I feel . . already . . as if I . . belong to you," Ilesa said in a whisper.

"You *do* belong to me," the Duke replied positively. "We are a part of each other and it is impossible for us now to be divided."

He turned her face up to his and kissed her again.

Now his kisses were gentle, as if he was wooing her into giving him her heart.

Rajah thought he was being neglected and drew attention to himself by rubbing himself against the Duke's legs.

Then he attempted to squeeze himself between them.

Ilesa gave a shaky little laugh.

"Rajah is . . jealous!" she said. "He is . . another who is . . trying to . . prevent us . . from being . . together."

"We will share Rajah," the Duke said, "and somehow, by some miracle, perhaps by prayer, we will find a way out of this maze into the Heaven which you have opened for me."

Ilesa looked up at him.

"You are . . so important," she said. "Are you . . certain that I am . . really the right person to be . . your wife?"

"You are the *only* person I have ever considered for that position," the Duke replied. "Just as my animals love and trust you, as they have never trusted anyone else but me, so my people at Heron, and on the other estates I own, need you and want you."

His arms tightened around her as he said:

"Oh, my Precious, do not let us have to wait very long."

"I do not . . know what to . . do," Ilesa said. "I love you . . I know that . . I love you . . but Doreen will be so . . angry and Papa will be . . so . . miserable."

Her voice broke on the last word and the Duke said:

"Now we will go and talk to Che-Che and perhaps he will tell us what we want to know."

He was trying in his own way to speak lightly and stop her from being so unhappy.

Because he understood and because her whole being seemed to respond to him, Ilesa allowed him to lead her out of Rajah's enclosure.

They walked hand-in-hand to Che-Che's.

He was waiting for them!

He sprang at the Duke in sheer delight as they entered his enclosure.

They talked to him and Me-Me came from her

hiding-place, moving out further than she had the day before.

She even allowed both the Duke and Ilesa to pat her.

"I am sure they understand what we are . . feeling," Ilesa said.

"Of course they do!" the Duke replied. "They know how lonely I have been at Heron without someone to share them with me."

Ilesa gave a little laugh.

"Now you are inventing a sad story for yourself!" she teased. "You know perfectly well you have had party after party here, parties in London, parties at Newmarket, and you have only to ask for something for it to be yours."

"I do not have to explain to you," the Duke said, "that parties are one thing and being with you is something very different. We think the same, we feel the same, and really, my precious, there is no need for words – is there?"

Ilesa knew this was true.

She was aware that she could share with him her thoughts as she had never shared them with anyone else.

For a moment they just looked at each other.

She could feel as if his lips were on hers the waves of ecstasy passing between them.

For a moment neither of them moved.

Then the Duke said:

"Exactly! How could anybody else ever understand – except you?"

Ilesa turned away with a little sob.

"If only . . you were not . . a Duke," she murmured.

She spoke tragically and the Duke gave a little laugh.

"But I am!" he said. "I am sorry, my Darling, but you will just have to put up with it, although I am quite prepared to admit that it is rather tiresome!"

Then suddenly they were both laughing.

The Duke was thinking that he had found the one woman in the world who really wanted him for himself.

For to Ilesa his title was a sheer disadvantage, together with all its pomp and circumstance.

The Duke looked at his watch.

"It feels as if we have been here only a few minutes," he said, "and I have so much more to say to you. But unless we want people to be aware of what is happening between us, I think we should return now to the house for breakfast."

"Yes . . of course," Ilesa agreed.

She kissed Che-Che on top of his head.

"You are a very clever cheetah," she said, "and I am sure you understand exactly what is happening."

"Of course he does," the Duke said, "and so does Rajah. I am certain they knew while I was sad and lonely here that you were somewhere in the world and they arranged in their own crafty little minds how I should find you."

Ilesa laughed.

"That would make a lovely story! One day you must write it down and I will illustrate it."

"That will certainly be something our children will enjoy!" the Duke said.

He waited to see the colour come into her cheeks, her eyes look shy.

Then he said:

"Oh, God, how much I love you! I will go on fighting for you, even if it kills me!"

CHAPTER SEVEN

Ilesa and the Duke patted Che-Che again and then walked towards the gate.

The cheetah followed them and Ilesa looked back.

"I think he knows we are worried," she said.

"I am sure he does," the Duke answered.

They shut the gate and started to walk quite quickly back through the Orchard.

When they reached the Herb-Garden, the Duke stopped.

"I think," he said, "we ought to go in separately."

"Of course, that is sensible," Ilesa agreed.

She thought how clever he was at thinking of everything and looked up at him with shining eyes.

"I love you," he said in a very deep voice, "and you know how much I am worrying at the moment in case you try to escape me."

"I will . . not do . . that," she said, "but . . ."

"I know. I know!" the Duke interrupted. "There is always a 'but'. But, Darling, do not keep me waiting too long."

He did not kiss her although she was hoping he would.

Then, as he turned to stand looking down into the fountain, she hurried away.

As she walked across the lawn she was praying that somehow by some miracle everything would solve itself.

"What can I do, Mama?" she asked in her heart. "What can I do? I know you are thinking of me, but you will also be thinking of Papa, and I cannot leave him alone when he is so unhappy."

She felt as if her prayer winged up to Heaven and her Mother was listening.

Then when she reached the house, instead of going round to the front door, she slipped through the french window into the Salon.

When she walked into the Breakfast-Room she found her Father was there with Lady Mavis and Lord Randall.

"Good morning, Papa," she said, kissing the Vicar.

"I thought you would be out riding," he said.

"I went into the garden," Ilesa said quickly, "and Papa you must look at the Herb-Garden. I know how thrilled Mama would have been if we could have had one like it."

The Vicar did not answer.

Ilesa walked to the sideboard where there was a long array of silver dishes.

As she reached it, Doreen came into the Dining-Room.

"I got up early," she announced before anybody could say anything, "because I think we must do

134

something very exciting this morning as you, Papa, will be leaving tomorrow."

There was a note in her voice which told Ilesa all too clearly that Doreen was anxious to be rid of them.

She was making it quite clear that their invitation was not to be extended any longer.

As she stood at the sideboard, Lord Randall was beside her.

"Let me help you," he said.

Then in a voice which only Doreen should have heard he said:

"You are looking very beautiful. Even more beautiful than you did last night."

"That makes me think that I must persuade Drogo to give a proper Ball here," Doreen answered.

Lord Randall did not speak.

Ilesa however, saw the pain in his eyes and thought that her sister again was being unnecessarily cruel.

They were all sitting at the table when the Duke came in.

"Good morning," he said. "I warn you all it is going to be very hot today, so we must choose our amusements where we will not sizzle in the heat."

"I thought," Lord Randall said before anyone else could speak, "that we might, Drogo, have a competition of jumping in the paddock. I have been inspecting those new fences you have put up and I think they are magnificent."

"I have taken a great deal of trouble over them,"

the Duke answered, "and it is certainly an idea that we might put some of the new horses at them."

"I do not like jumping," Doreen said petulantly.

There was a pause before the Duke said:

"But of course, Doreen, you must be the judge and you shall give away the prizes."

"What prizes?" Doreen enquired.

"That will be a surprise," the Duke replied, "and I will think of something really exciting for the participants – and of course the Judge."

Ilesa realised by the way her Sister preened herself that she thought the Duke had promised something more important than just surprise.

Then the Butler came to the Duke's side.

"I thought, Your Grace," he said, "you would like to know that Hilton has just brought in the white orchids that Your Grace brought back from Singapore. They have been arranged in a bowl and I have put them in the Salon on the table by the window."

"My orchids from Singapore!" the Duke exclaimed. "I was hoping they would come into bloom. Tell Hilton I am delighted to have them."

"Very good, Your Grace."

The Butler withdrew and Lady Mavis said:

"They have come on quickly in the heat. I looked at them the day before yesterday, and they were not yet in bloom."

"I did the same," the Duke said. "But I want you all to see them because they are a very rare and unusual orchid and pure white."

He glanced at Ilesa as he spoke.

She knew, because she could read his thoughts

that he was thinking it was what she was to him – pure and white.

She looked down at her plate in case she should blush and someone might notice it.

She was not aware that the Duke looked away from her with difficulty.

When he had finished his breakfast, he realised that because he had come in late everyone else had finished too.

"Now," he said, "let us go to look at the orchids. I am sure you will think, as I did when I saw them, that they are exceptional and quite the most beautiful flower imaginable."

He opened the door.

Doreen and Ilesa walked through it, he and Lord Randall followed them.

The Vicar and Lady Mavis were a little longer rising from the Breakfast-Table.

The others walked across the hall and into the Salon.

The sun was streaming through a window and at the far end of the room Ilesa could see the flowers on a table in front of the window.

Then as she and her sister walked towards it, Doreen suddenly gave a shriek.

It was so loud and so shrill that Ilesa stared at her in astonishment.

She shrieked again.

Then Ilesa was aware that Che-Che had just come in through the french window and was standing, staring at them.

Doreen turned round and ran towards the two men who were standing behind her.

She flung herself against Lord Randall saying:

"Hugo! Hugo! Save me . . save . . me!"

His arms went round her.

As she trembled against him, he said:

"I will take care of you, my Darling."

Ilesa ran towards Che-Che, but the Duke was looking at Doreen in the arms of Lord Randall.

Her face was hidden in his neck and his arms held her very close against his chest.

"It looks, Hugo," the Duke said quietly, "as if I should congratulate you."

"I hope so, Drogo," Lord Randall replied.

Then he picked Doreen up in his arms and carried her across the room to where an open door led into an Ante-Chamber.

Ilesa was crouching down beside Che-Che with her arms around him.

As the Duke joined her, she said:

"I knew Che-Che was worried about us, and that is why he has escaped."

The Duke drew a deep breath of relief.

"That has solved one problem for us at any rate," he said, "and Hugo will be happy."

Ilesa looked at him in surprise.

"You knew he was in love with Doreen?"

"It was only very recently that I suspected it, and that he was serious about it."

"I think," Ilesa said in a low tone, "Doreen was really in love with him all the time, but she was hypnotised by the glamour of the strawberry leaves on your Coronet."

The Duke's eyes twinkled.

"I promise you, my Precious," he said, "I will wear it only on very formal occasions."

Ilesa smiled, but she did not answer him.

He knew she was thinking of her Father.

Even if Doreen no longer stood in the way of their being together, there was still the Vicar to be considered.

"I love you," the Duke said softly.

. . . .

The Vicar and Lady Mavis had been following the rest of the party into the Salon when the Butler stopped them.

"Excuse me, Sir," he said to the Vicar, "but I think you should look at the Morning Papers which have just arrived. They are in His Lordship's Study."

The way he spoke in a deep serious tone made the Vicar look at him in surprise.

At the same time he did not ask any questions.

Lady Mavis had heard what the Butler said.

As the Vicar turned and went down the corridor towards the Study, she went with him.

They neither of them spoke.

The Vicar opened the door and they went into the room.

The Vicar walked straight to the stool in front of the fireplace.

The Morning Papers were always laid out there neatly.

He picked up *"The Morning Post"*.

As he looked at the front page he gave a gasp.

The headlines seemed to spring out at him:

BRITISH SOLDIERS AMBUSHED BY TRIBESMEN.

A MASSACRE ON THE NORTH-WEST FRONTIER.

The Governor of the North-West Frontier Province, the Earl of Harlestone, and his only son, shot dead.

The Vicar read the headlines and Lady Mavis standing behind him read them too.

She put her hand on his arm as she said:

"I am so sorry."

"And I am sorry for my Sister-in-Law," the Vicar said quietly. "I must of course, get in touch with our other relations."

He was talking as if to himself.

Then Lady Mavis said:

"Of course you must do that. It will be up to you to make all the arrangements for the bodies to be brought back and buried in the Family Vault."

The Vicar looked at her and she said:

"You must realise that you are now the head of the family and The Earl of Harlestone."

She knew as she spoke that it had not struck the Vicar that that was his position until she had pointed it out to him.

Then looking at her, he drew in his breath before he said very quietly:

"Now I can beg you to do me the very great honour of being my wife."

Their eyes met and Lady Mavis gave a little cry.

"I was so afraid," she said, "that you would not ask me."

The Vicar put out his arms and she moved closer to him.

. . . .

In the Salon one of the Indians who looked after the Duke's menagerie appeared at the window.

He was obviously out of breath having been running as fast as he could.

When he saw the Duke he salaamed.

"Forgive, Lord Sahib," he said. "Che-Che slip by ver-ry quick as I go in – pen. I run ver-ry fast but not catch."

"He is quite safe here," the Duke replied. "And I think, in fact, he was looking for me and Miss Harle."

"Che-Che love you ver-ry much, Lord Sahib," the Indian answered.

As he spoke he clasped a collar round Che-Che's neck and attached to it a leather leading-rein.

"We will come to see you later," Ilesa said, patting Che-Che as he was led away.

"You were quite right," she said to the Duke. "Che-Che knew that we wanted him, and he was very clever to find us."

"I think you drew him to you by your magic," the Duke answered, "just as you have drawn me."

They had both risen to their feet.

The Duke was putting out his arms towards her when he heard someone come into the room.

As he moved to one side, he realised it was the Butler.

"What is it?" he asked.

"I thought Your Grace should know," the Butler said, "that there is bad news for His Reverence the Vicar in the Morning Papers."

"Bad news?" the Duke questioned.

"Yes, Your Grace. The Earl of Harlestone and his only son have been shot in a rising in India."

"Good gracious!" the Duke exclaimed.

"The Vicar and Her Ladyship are in the Study, Your Grace."

The Butler moved away.

When they were alone in the Salon, Ilesa said:

"Oh, poor Papa. He will be so upset!"

"Of course he will," the Duke agreed. "At the same time, he is now 'rich Papa'."

Ilesa looked at him, and he said:

"You must realise your Father is now The Earl of Harlestone!"

"Yes, I suppose so," Ilesa said in a wondering voice. "Oh, Drogo! That means he can now employ again all the people who were dismissed when Uncle Robert went to India."

There was a sudden lilt in her voice as she spoke.

The Duke wondered how many other women would be thinking of those who were unemployed rather than the difference her Father's position would now make to herself.

"We must go to Papa at once," Ilesa said.

"Of course," the Duke agreed.

They walked from the Salon and down the corridor.

The Duke opened the door of the Study.

As Ilesa walked in she saw to her astonishment that her Father had his arms round Lady Mavis.

For a moment she could only stare at them.

Then before she could speak the Duke said:

"We have been told, Vicar, that you have had shocking news about your Brother. At the same time I feel sure that no one could take over the position he left behind in England better than yourself."

"Thank you," the Vicar said quietly. "I think I should tell Your Grace that I shall be supported in the position about which you speak by your Aunt."

He smiled at Lady Mavis as he spoke.

Ilesa thought she had not seen her Father look so happy or so carefree since her Mother's death.

"Do you mean, Papa," she asked, "that Lady Mavis is going to marry you?"

"She has done me that very great honour," the Vicar replied, "and I know how much she will help me with all the difficulties which lie ahead."

Ilesa knew what he was thinking of.

There would be the restoration of the house, the people to be re-employed and the whole Estate to be brought back to prosperity!

Then the Duke took charge.

"I want to make some suggestions which I think

143

will be to the advantage, not only of His Lordship, but of the rest of us."

The three people to whom he was speaking looked at him in surprise and he went on:

"First, I would like the new Earl of Harlestone to marry me to his daughter within the next few hours."

The Vicar gave a gasp, but the Duke continued:

"I think once we have left on our honeymoon, it would be very wise if my Aunt and the Earl were married also today, before they return to Littlestone."

It was now Lady Mavis's turn to look astonished until the Duke explained:

"If you wait until the Family and everyone else learns of Robert Harle's death, they will know that you are in mourning, and that your marriage must be postponed."

He glanced at Ilesa before he added:

"I have heard all about the problems that are waiting for you, and I feel that you need the support and assistance of my Aunt which she would not be able to give if you were not already married. You can be married perfectly legally simply as Mark Harle."

The Vicar drew in a deep breath.

"But of course," he said, "you are right. Do you agree, Mavis my dear, to your Nephew's very sensible, in fact brilliant, suggestion?"

"But of course I do," Lady Mavis said. "I want to help you. You know I want to do that."

Ilesa knew by the way she spoke, that she was very much in love with her Father.

She thought that nothing could be better.

Nothing would make him happier than to have someone so kind, gentle and understanding beside him.

As if they had all agreed the Duke said:

"Now I will send at once for my private Chaplain, and shall we say, Vicar, that you will marry me and your daughter at precisely eleven thirty?"

Ilesa gave a little cry.

"I want to marry you. Of course, I want to marry you! But have you realised that as your wife I have nothing to wear?"

The Duke gave a little laugh.

"In which case, my Darling," he said, "we will start our honeymoon in Paris. I will dress you in a way which will make your beauty even more over-whelming than it is at the moment. At the same time, as I shall be a very jealous husband, I am rather sorry that I cannot insist on your wearing a yashmak."

They all laughed and the Vicar said:

"I feel as if I am being swept off my feet by a flood-tide! But I am not complaining! I am sure, Drogo, that you are right in what you have suggested."

"Now I will put the wheels in motion," the Duke said, "and we must drink to our happiness. But, as it is only just after Breakfast, a little later in the day."

He walked out of the Study as he spoke, and Ilesa went to her Father and kissed him.

"I am so happy for you, Papa," she said. "Now

you will have enough money to do all the things you have always wanted to do, and we no longer need to know the cottages are falling down, and the people in Littlestone feeling half-starved."

"And I know you, my Dear, will be very happy," the Vicar replied. "I have the greatest admiration for Drogo, and Lady Mavis has been telling me how unhappy he was when he was a little boy and lost his Mother."

"I will try to make it up to him," Ilesa said.

Both she and her Father knew it was a vow.

When she went upstairs to her bedroom to tell the Maid to pack she found that the Duke's news had already percolated through the house.

The Housekeeper and two Maids were already packing what clothes she had with her.

But with the exception of course, of her Mother's Wedding-Dress.

"Am I to wear that?" she asked the Housekeeper.

"But of course, Miss," the elderly woman replied, "and I have the veil that Her Grace wore at her Wedding. The tiaras have been brought from the safe. So you can make a choice of which you think suits you the best."

Ilesa looked a little bewildered and the House-keeper went on:

"This is a happy day for all of us, Miss. We have been hoping that His Grace would bring home a bride who would fill his Mother's place and whom we would all like."

Mrs. Field took a breath before she continued:

"I speak for myself and all the household, when I

146

tell you truthfully, Miss, that you are just the bride we hoped His Grace would choose."

Ilesa said:

"Thank you very much. I know that you all will try to help me and prevent me from making mistakes. I have never lived in such a big house as this, but I want to make it a happy home for my husband."

She spoke a little shyly.

The old Housekeeper blinked away her tears before she replied:

"And now, Miss, we have to think of what you can go away in. His Grace told me he was taking you to Paris, but you have not much to put on before you get there."

"That is true," Ilesa said. "It would be very kind if you could again lend me something."

It flashed through her mind that she might appeal to her Sister.

Then she realised that they had in fact, forgotten Doreen who might make difficulties.

She would certainly not be pleased at her marrying the Duke.

Then because she was so happy, Ilesa tried not to think of Doreen's disapproval.

"I am sure she will be happy with Lord Randall," she tried to tell herself.

But she was still a little apprehensive.

Mrs. Field found several pretty gowns which, although a little out-of-date, were certainly very becoming.

"I wish we had more time," she said. "But His

Grace has always been in a hurry ever since I've known him. Though I never expected a Wedding with literally only a few minutes to spare!"

Ilesa laughed.

"I shall be very grateful for these gowns," she said. "They are certainly very much smarter than anything I possess myself."

She in fact hardly looked at the dresses before the Maid put them into a trunk.

It was a new one which Mrs. Field had provided for her.

It was so wonderful that after all her anxiety she could now marry the Duke without feeling guilty, and without, she hoped, hurting anyone.

Finally she was dressed in her Mother's Wedding-Gown, and her hair was arranged in the latest fashion and covered with an exquisite Brussels lace veil.

Mrs. Field asked her which of the tiaras, which had been laid out on the bed, she would like to wear.

She chose the smallest.

It was the least overpowering and also to her the most beautiful.

It represented an arrangement of flowers all done in diamonds.

When Ilesa looked at herself in the mirror she knew the Duke would approve of what she had chosen.

To him she was a flower, and she must never fade.

She knew also that he had placed her in the shrine that was hidden in his heart.

One minute before 11.30 the Housekeeper opened the Bedroom door.

"His Grace'll be waiting for you in the Hall, Miss," she said. "May God Bless you and bring you both great happiness on this the most important day of your lives."

"Thank you! Thank you," Ilesa said.

The Maids wished her good luck as she walked slowly along the corridor and down the great staircase to the Hall.

The Duke was waiting.

She thought that she had never seen him look so magnificent.

The front of his cutaway coat was ablaze with his decorations and he wore The Order of The Garter over one shoulder.

He waited until Ilesa reached the last step of the staircase.

Then he put out his hands and took hers.

"You look, my Darling," he said in a low voice, "exactly as I wanted you to look. Like an angel coming down from Heaven to help, protect and guide me."

Ilesa's fingers tightened on his and he said:

"This is how I always wanted to be married. Without a crowd, sniggering and giggling. With just you and the people we love."

"I feel I am dreaming," Ilesa said. "Can this really be true?"

"I will make it true later in the day when you are really my wife," the Duke replied.

He picked up a bouquet which was lying on a side-table.

As she took it Ilesa realised it was composed of the white orchids which he had found in Singapore.

She thought they were not only a sign of his love, but had also brought them both the luck they had never expected.

If after Breakfast they had not gone into the Salon to look at the orchids, no one would have known that Che-Che had found his way there.

Doreen would not have been frightened by him into Hugo's arms.

It was as if everything had been directed in some clever way from Heaven.

Ilesa sent up a little prayer of thanks to her Mother.

As they walked along the corridor the Duke said:

"Just in case, my Darling, it is worrying you. Doreen and Hugo have already left Heron."

Ilesa looked up at him in surprise and he explained:

"Hugo is taking no chances! She has promised to marry him, and they left for London, driving my new Team so that they will get there quickly."

"That was very kind of you," Ilesa said.

The Duke gave a little laugh.

"I would have given Hugo all my horses and half Heron itself to know that you were no longer concerned about your Sister. She will, I am sure, be very happy with Hugo who adores her."

"I am happy that . . no one is now . . resenting our . . marriage and I am so . . very . . very lucky that I can . . marry . . you."

"And what do you think I feel?" the Duke enquired.

He looked down at her, and then said very softly:

"I will tell you what I feel later, when you are really and truly mine."

As they neared the Chapel there was the sound of music being played very softly.

They went in through the Gothic doorway.

Ilesa saw that her Father, wearing a magnificent vestment, was waiting for them.

She realised too that, in the very short time that had been available, masses of flowers had been brought into the Chapel.

With the candles lit and with the sunshine coming in through the stained-glass window the whole place was very beautiful.

There was the Duke's Chaplain to help Ilesa's Father marry them.

The only other witness was Lady Mavis who was sitting in one of the carved pews.

Ilesa thought that she had never heard her Father read the Service more movingly.

At the same time there was an undoubted happiness in his voice, that she had missed the last two years.

Then finally she and the Duke knelt and he blessed them.

Ilesa thought she could hear the angels singing and that her Mother was looking down at them.

She was smiling because it was what she had wanted.

"Thank you! Thank . . you!" Ilesa said in her

heart. "And thank You . . God. Please help me to make Drogo happy, and everyone else with whom I am now concerned."

It was a prayer that was so intense that it brought tears to her eyes.

Then as they rose to their feet the Duke very gently lifted her veil and threw it back over her head.

He kissed her.

It was a kiss of dedication and told her that the vows he had just taken were very sacred.

He would keep them to the end of his life.

. . . .

The Duke arranged that the moment Ilesa had changed they should leave and not attend her Father's marriage to Lady Mavis.

"I think they would like to be alone," the Duke said. "Therefore I have given orders that they should have luncheon here. Then a carriage will take them to Harlestone Hall."

"You have thought of everything," Ilesa murmured.

"I have thought of you," the Duke answered, "and I want to make certain, my Precious, that you think of me, and only of me – so actually I am very selfish."

Ilesa knew that this was far from the truth.

She was well aware that it was because he thought of his people, just as he thought of his horses and his animals, that everyone at Heron was happy.

As they drove down the drive Ilesa said:

"I think we ought to have said goodbye to Che-Che and thanked him for being so clever as to reach us just when we needed him."

"We will thank him when we come home," the Duke replied, "and I thought we should bring back from our honeymoon some additions to the menagerie."

Ilesa clasped her hands together and looked at him with shining eyes.

"What are you thinking of," she asked.

"That is something we can discuss together," he said. "I thought when we have bought your trousseau in Paris, my yacht will be waiting for us in the Mediterranean. We could visit Cairo and perhaps go down the Red Sea to the Gulf."

He paused to smile at her before he continued:

"There are many strange species of animals and birds which I think we should have at home. But of course I am prepared to leave the choice to you."

"Oh, Drogo, what a wonderful idea!" Ilesa cried. "It will be very .. very .. exciting to have a menagerie which we can add to whenever we go away, and where of course, Rajah and Che-Che will always be there to welcome us home."

She sounded so excited and thrilled at the idea.

The Duke thought he had never expected to share a menagerie with his wife.

No man could be as fortunate as he was.

They stayed the night in a house the Duke owned.

It was half-way between Heron and a quiet cove in which his yacht would be waiting for them the following day.

It was a very attractive little Tudor house set in a garden of roses and lavender.

It had belonged, the Duke told her, before she married, to his Mother's family.

"There were other big houses, several of them. But this is the one I kept," he said. "Every time that I have stayed here by myself, I thought that one day I might bring my wife."

"Now . . I am here," Ilesa murmured.

"Do you think I am not aware of that?" he asked.

There was a look in his eyes that made her feel shy.

When she went up to change for dinner she found there was an old Housemaid to look after her.

She had known the Duke when he was a little boy.

"A nicer young man there 'as never been, Yer Grace," she said. "We loved 'im, and of'en talked of who 'e'd marry. Us 'oped it'd be someone who really loved 'im."

Ilesa smiled and the old Housemaid went on:

"Yer're very beautiful, Yer Grace, and I knows as soon as I saw ye that yer beauty was not only in yer face but in yer heart, and that's wot we were 'oping for!"

Ilesa felt like crying because it was so touching.

She realised at dinner exactly how much the Duke was loved by the old people.

Although they had only been told an hour or so earlier that the Duke was coming, the dinner was superb.

The gardeners had decorated the table with white

154

flowers, and there were vases of them all over the house.

When dinner was over Ilesa expected to go into the very attractive Drawing-Room, but the Duke said:

"It has been an exciting day, my Darling, and I do not want you to be too tired tomorrow."

"I do not feel tired," Ilesa answered. "I feel as if I am dancing in the sky, which was what I felt when you danced with me the first time."

"We will dance when we reach Paris," the Duke promised, "but now my precious, I want to teach you about love."

They went into their Bedroom, which had an old fashioned four-poster bed.

There was the scent of lavender coming from the lace-edged sheets.

The fragrance of roses came in through the windows, from those climbing up the outside of the house.

There was no one else there.

The Duke shut the door.

Then he came across the room and put his arms around Ilesa.

"How can this really have happened?" he asked. "I thought I might have to wait and fight for you for years. Now thanks to the gods, and of course, Che-Che, you are already mine. Mine, really mine! I do not have to wait any longer."

Having finished speaking his lips were on Ilesa's.

He kissed her at first gently.

Then more and more passionately, so that she felt

as if she melted into him, and was no longer herself but a part of him.

Then she felt him very gently undoing her Mother's Wedding-Gown.

She had worn it again tonight, because he had asked that she should.

"You look more lovely in it," he said, "than in anything I could possibly buy you in Paris. We will keep it my Darling, and you shall wear it on every anniversary so that we will never forget the wonder of our Wedding Day."

As it slipped from Ilesa's shoulders and slithered down on to the floor, the Duke picked her up into his arms.

He carried her to the big four-poster bed.

He laid her down very gently on the pillows.

She realised that he was blowing out the lights one by one.

Then he pulled back the curtains.

The moonlight streamed in like a silver cloud.

She could see the stars twinkling like diamonds in the sky.

A few seconds later he was beside her, and he drew her into his arms.

She knew then that her Fairy Story had not ended as she had expected, but had just begun.

It was a Fairy Story so beautiful, so rapturous that she knew that she was no longer tied to the ordinary world.

She was floating in a Paradise where there were no problems and misery, but only happiness.

"I love you," the Duke said in a deep voice. "I

love you from the top of your golden head to the soles of your little feet. You are mine, my Darling, from now until eternity."

"I love . . you! I love . . you for . . eternity," Ilesa answered.

Then as the Duke made her his, she knew it was true.

Their love was so deep, so magical, so perfect that it would be with them not only for this life, but many lives to come.

It was Eternal and came from God.

. . . .

Che-Che stretched himself out on the soft ground beneath the bush. Me-Me nestled close to him.

All the way back from the house the Indian had scolded him in fluent Urdu for running away.

"You bad Che-Che, go off quick. Lord Sahib ver-ry angry wi' you."

Che-Che knew Lord Sahib was not angry but pleased with him, and Mem-Sahib loved him.

He felt it in the touch of her hands and in the sound of her voice.

When he saw her again he would nibble her ear.

Other books by Barbara Cartland

Romantic Novels, over 500, the most recently published being:

Lucky Logan Finds Love
Born of Love
The Angel and the Rake
The Queen of Hearts
The Wicked Widow
To Scotland and Love
Love and War
Love at the Ritz
The Dangerous Marriage
Good, Or Bad?
The Dream and the Glory

This is Love
Seek the Stars
Running Away to Love
Look with the Heart
Safe in Paradise
Love in the Ruins
A Coronation of Love
A Duel of Jewels
The Duke is Trapped
The Wonderful Dream

(In aid of the St. John Ambulance Brigade)

Autobiographical and Biographical:

The Isthmus Years 1919–1939
The Years of Opportunity 1939–1945
I Search for Rainbows 1945–1976
We Danced All Night 1919–1929
Ronald Cartland (With a foreword by Sir Winston Churchill)
Polly – My Wonderful Mother
I Seek the Miraculous

Historical:

Bewitching Women
The Outrageous Queen (The Story of Queen Christina of Sweden)
The Scandalous Life of King Carol
The Private Life of Charles II
The Private Life of Elizabeth, Empress of Austria
Josephine, Empress of France
Diane de Poitiers
Metternich – The Passionate Diplomat
A Year of Royal Days
Royal Jewels
Royal Eccentrics
Royal Lovers

Sociology:

You in the Home	Etiquette
The Fascinating Forties	The Many Facets of Love
Marriage for Moderns	Sex and the Teenager
Be Vivid, Be Vital	The Book of Charm
Love, Life and Sex	Living Together
Vitamins for Vitality	The Youth Secret
Husbands and Wives	The Magic of Honey
Men are Wonderful	The Book of Beauty and Health

Keep Young and Beautiful by Barbara Cartland and Elinor Glyn
Etiquette for Love and Romance
Barbara Cartland's Book of Health

General:

Barbara Cartland's Book of Useless Information with a
   Foreword by the Earl Mountbatten of Burma.
   (In aid of the United World Colleges)
Love and Lovers (Picture Book)
The Light of Love (Prayer Book)
Barbara Cartland's Scrapbook
   (In aid of the Royal Photographic Museum)
Romantic Royal Marriages
Barbara Cartland's Book of Celebrities
Getting Older, Growing Younger

Verse:

Lines on Life and Love

Music:

An Album of Love Songs
sung with the Royal Philharmonic Orchestra.

Films:

A Hazard of Hearts
The Lady and the Highwayman
A Ghost in Monte Carlo
A Duel of Hearts

Cartoons:

Barbara Cartland Romances (Book of Cartoons)
has recently been published in the U.S.A., Great Britain,
and other parts of the world.

Children:

A Children's Pop-Up Book: "Princess to the Rescue"

Cookery:

Barbara Cartland's Health Food Cookery Book
Food for Love
Magic of Honey Cookbook
Recipes for Lovers
The Romance of Food

Editor of:

"The Common Problem" by Ronald Cartland (with a preface by
  the Rt. Hon. the Earl of Selborne, P.C.)
Barbara Cartland's Library of Love
  Library of Ancient Wisdom
"Written with Love" Passionate love letters selected by Barbara
  Cartland

Drama:

Blood Money
French Dressing

Philosophy:

Touch the Stars

Radio Operetta:

The Rose and the Violet
(Music by Mark Lubbock) Performed in 1942.

Radio Plays:

The Caged Bird: An episode in the life of Elizabeth Empress of
Austria. Performed in 1957.